ACCLAIM FOR JEFF SMITH'S

Named an all-time top ten graphic novel by **Time** *magazine.*

"As sweeping as the 'Lord of the Rings' cycle, but much funnier."   **—Andrew Arnold, Time.com**

★*"This is first-class kid lit: exciting, funny, scary, and resonant enough that it will stick with readers for a long time."*   **—Publishers Weekly,** *starred review*

"One of the best kids' comics ever."   **—Vibe** *magazine*

*"***BONE** *is storytelling at its best, full of endearing, flawed characters whose adventures run the gamut from hilarious whimsy . . . to thrilling drama."*   **—Entertainment Weekly**

"[This] sprawling, mythic comic is spectacular."   **—SPIN** *magazine*

"Jeff Smith's cartoons are irresistible. Every gorgeous sweep of his brush speaks volumes."   **—Frank Miller, creator of Sin City**

"Jeff Smith can pace a joke better than almost anyone in comics." —Neil Gaiman, author of **Coraline**

"I love BONE! BONE is great!"
  —Matt Groening, creator of **The Simpsons**

"Every one of the zillion characters has a unique set of personality traits and flaws and dreams that are developed amid the pandemonium."
  —Kyle Baker, **Plastic Man** cartoonist

"BONE moves from brash humor to gripping adventure in a single panel." —ALA **Booklist**

"BONE is a comic-book sensation. . . . [It] is a classic of writer-artist craftsmanship not to be missed."
  —Comics Buyer's Guide

OTHER *BONE* BOOKS

Out from Boneville

The Great Cow Race

Eyes of the Storm

The Dragonslayer

Rock Jaw: Master of the Eastern Border

OLD MAN'S CAVE

BY JEFF SMITH

WITH COLOR BY STEVE HAMAKER

An Imprint of

SCHOLASTIC

Library of Congress Catalog Card Number 9568403.
ISBN-13 978-0-439-70628-5 — ISBN-10 0-439-70628-9 (hardcover)
ISBN 0-439-70635-1 (paperback)

ACKNOWLEDGMENTS
Harvestar Family Crest designed by Charles Vess
Map of *The Valley* by Mark Crilley
Color by Steve Hamaker

30 29 28 27 26 25 24 23 22   17 18 19
First Scholastic edition, August 2007
Book design by David Saylor
Printed in Malaysia 108
Scholastic Inc., 557 Broadway, New York, NY 10012.

This book is for Jim Kammerud

CONTENTS

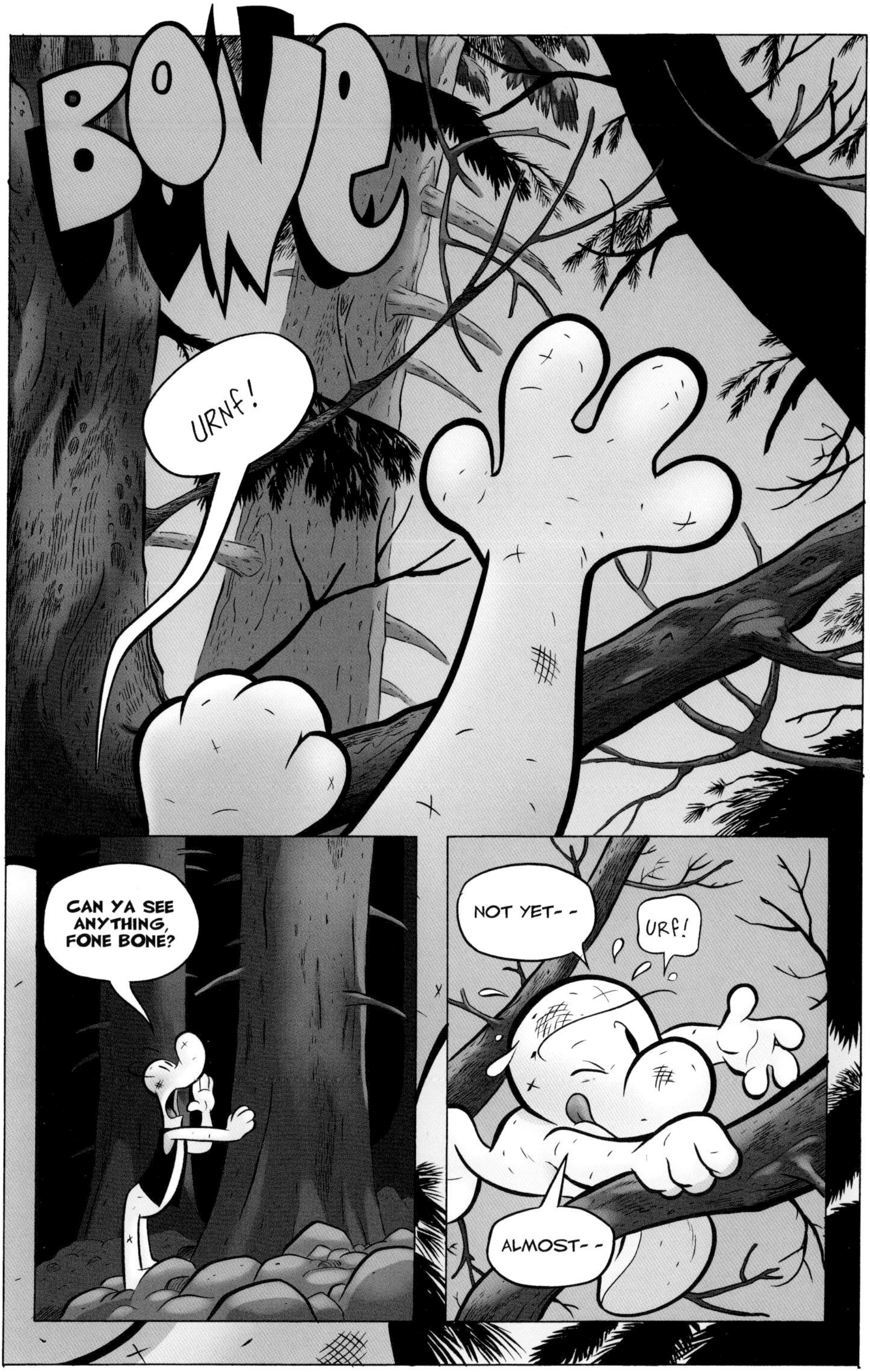
BONE
URNf!
CAN YA SEE ANYTHING, FONE BONE?
NOT YET- -
URf!
ALMOST- -

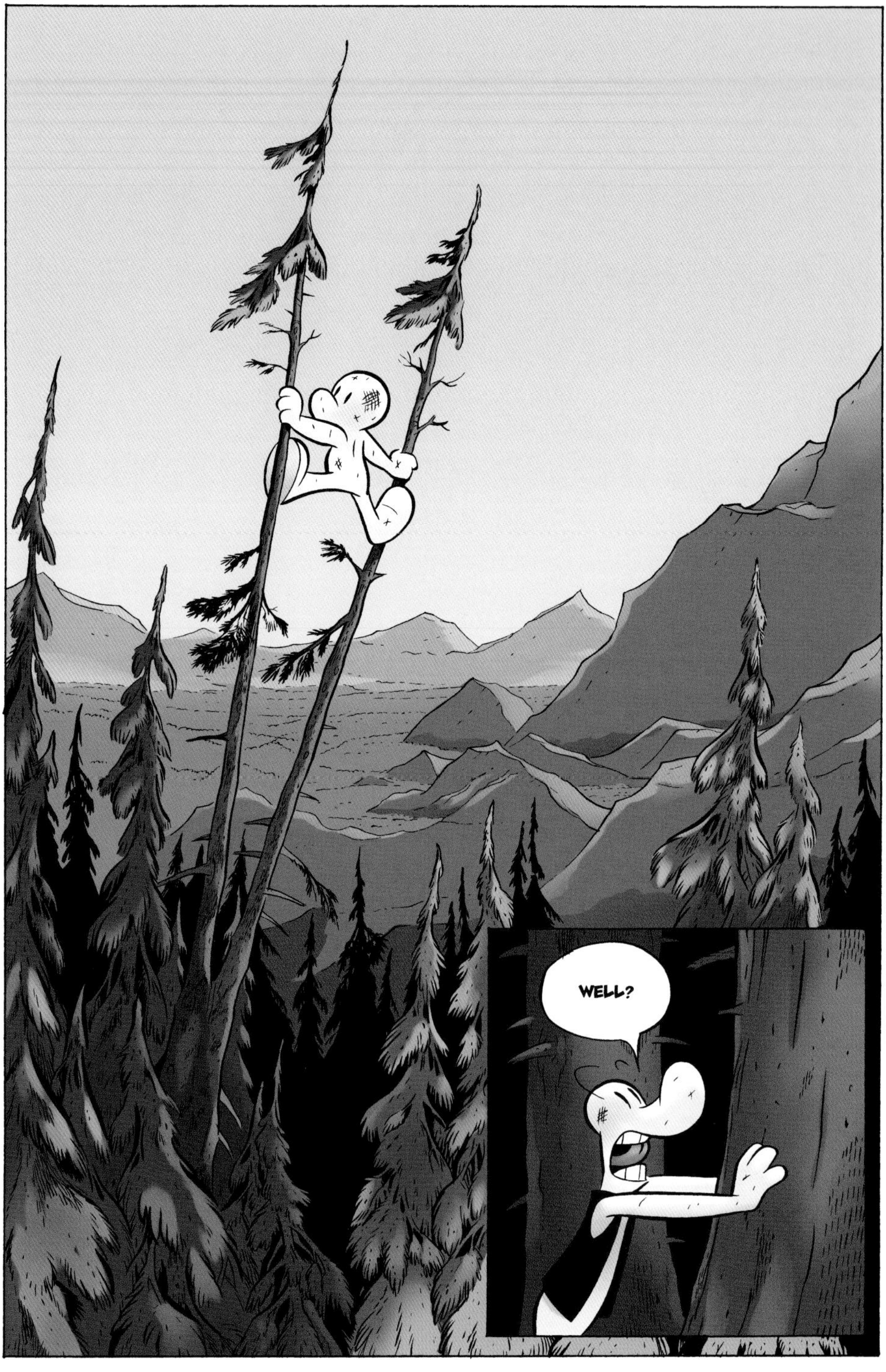
WELL?

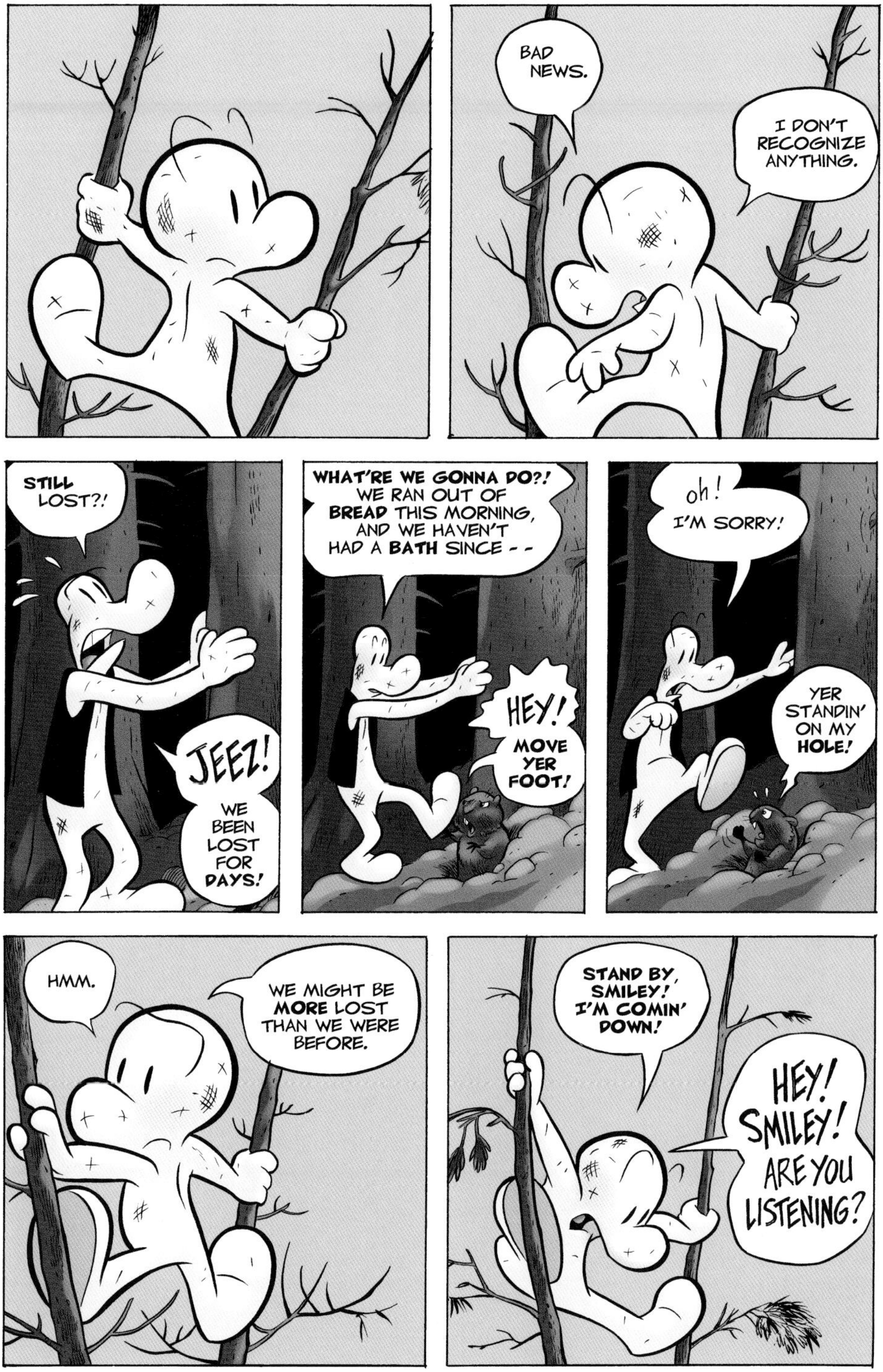
BAD NEWS.
I DON'T RECOGNIZE ANYTHING.
STILL LOST?!
JEEZ!
WE BEEN LOST FOR DAYS!
WHAT'RE WE GONNA DO?! WE RAN OUT OF BREAD THIS MORNING, AND WE HAVEN'T HAD A BATH SINCE - -
HEY!
MOVE YER FOOT!
oh! I'M SORRY!
YER STANDIN' ON MY HOLE!
HMM.
WE MIGHT BE MORE LOST THAN WE WERE BEFORE.
STAND BY, SMILEY! I'M COMIN' DOWN!
HEY! SMILEY! ARE YOU LISTENING?

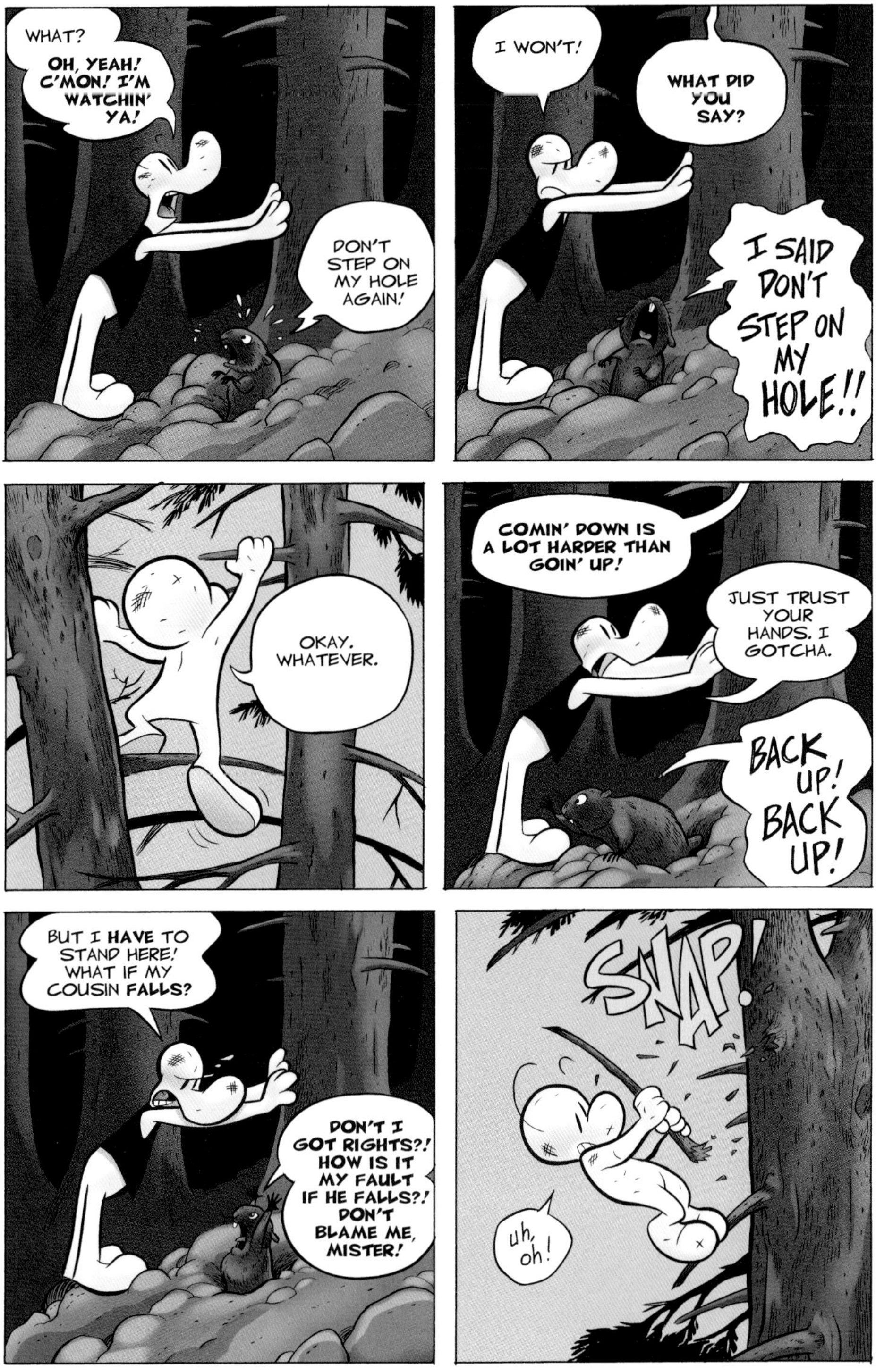
WHAT?
OH, YEAH! C'MON! I'M WATCHIN' YA!
DON'T STEP ON MY HOLE AGAIN!
I WON'T!
WHAT DID YOU SAY?
I SAID DON'T STEP ON MY HOLE!!
OKAY. WHATEVER.
COMIN' DOWN IS A LOT HARDER THAN GOIN' UP!
JUST TRUST YOUR HANDS. I GOTCHA.
BACK UP! BACK UP!
BUT I HAVE TO STAND HERE! WHAT IF MY COUSIN FALLS?
DON'T I GOT RIGHTS?! HOW IS IT MY FAULT IF HE FALLS?! DON'T BLAME ME, MISTER!
SNAP!
uh, oh!

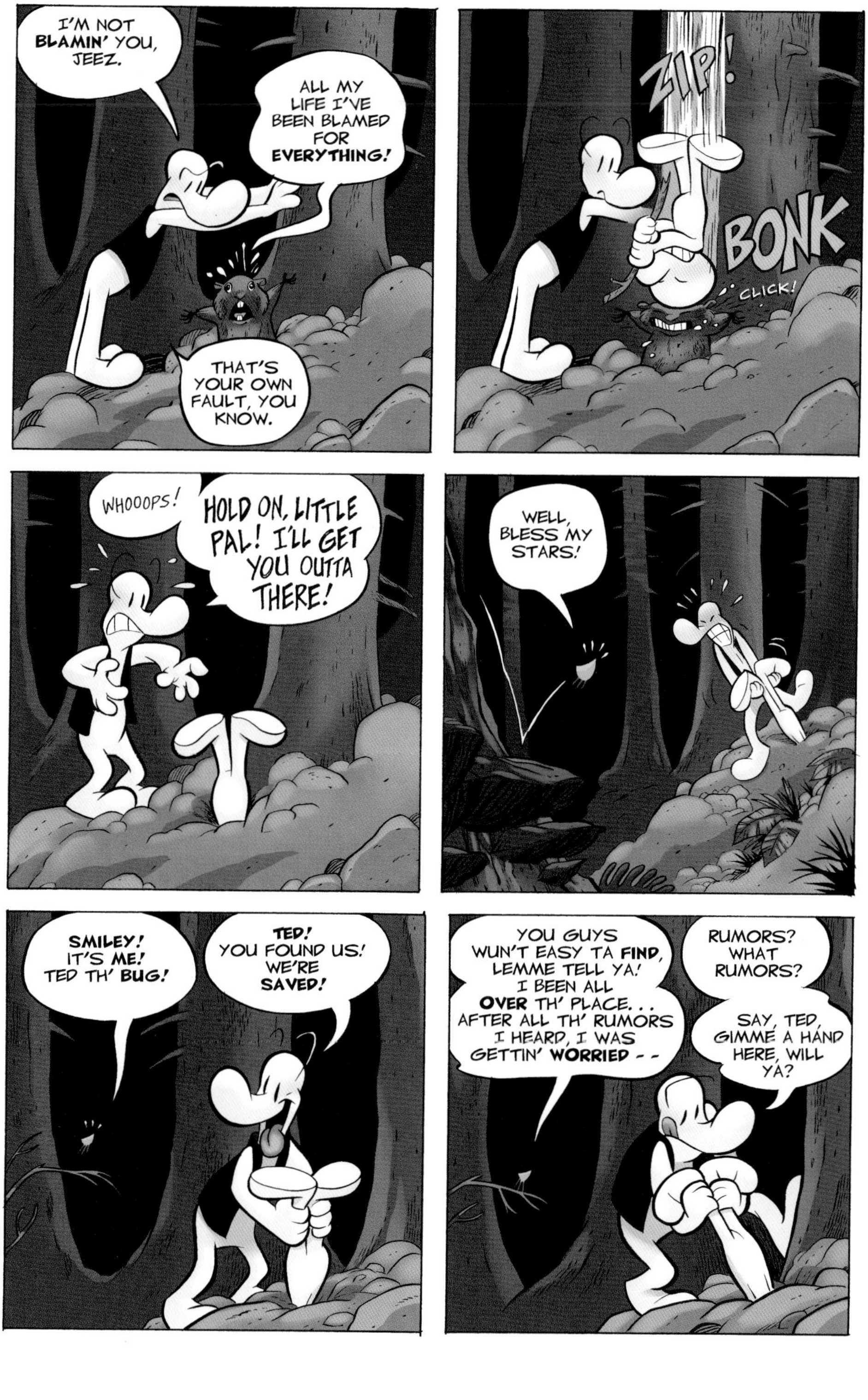
I'M NOT BLAMIN' YOU, JEEZ.
ALL MY LIFE I'VE BEEN BLAMED FOR EVERYTHING!
THAT'S YOUR OWN FAULT, YOU KNOW.
ZIP!
BONK
CLICK!
WHOOOPS!
HOLD ON, LITTLE PAL! I'LL GET YOU OUTTA THERE!
WELL, BLESS MY STARS!
SMILEY! IT'S ME! TED TH' BUG!
TED! YOU FOUND US! WE'RE SAVED!
YOU GUYS WUN'T EASY TA FIND, LEMME TELL YA! I BEEN ALL OVER TH' PLACE. . . AFTER ALL TH' RUMORS I HEARD, I WAS GETTIN' WORRIED - -
RUMORS? WHAT RUMORS?
SAY, TED, GIMME A HAND HERE, WILL YA?

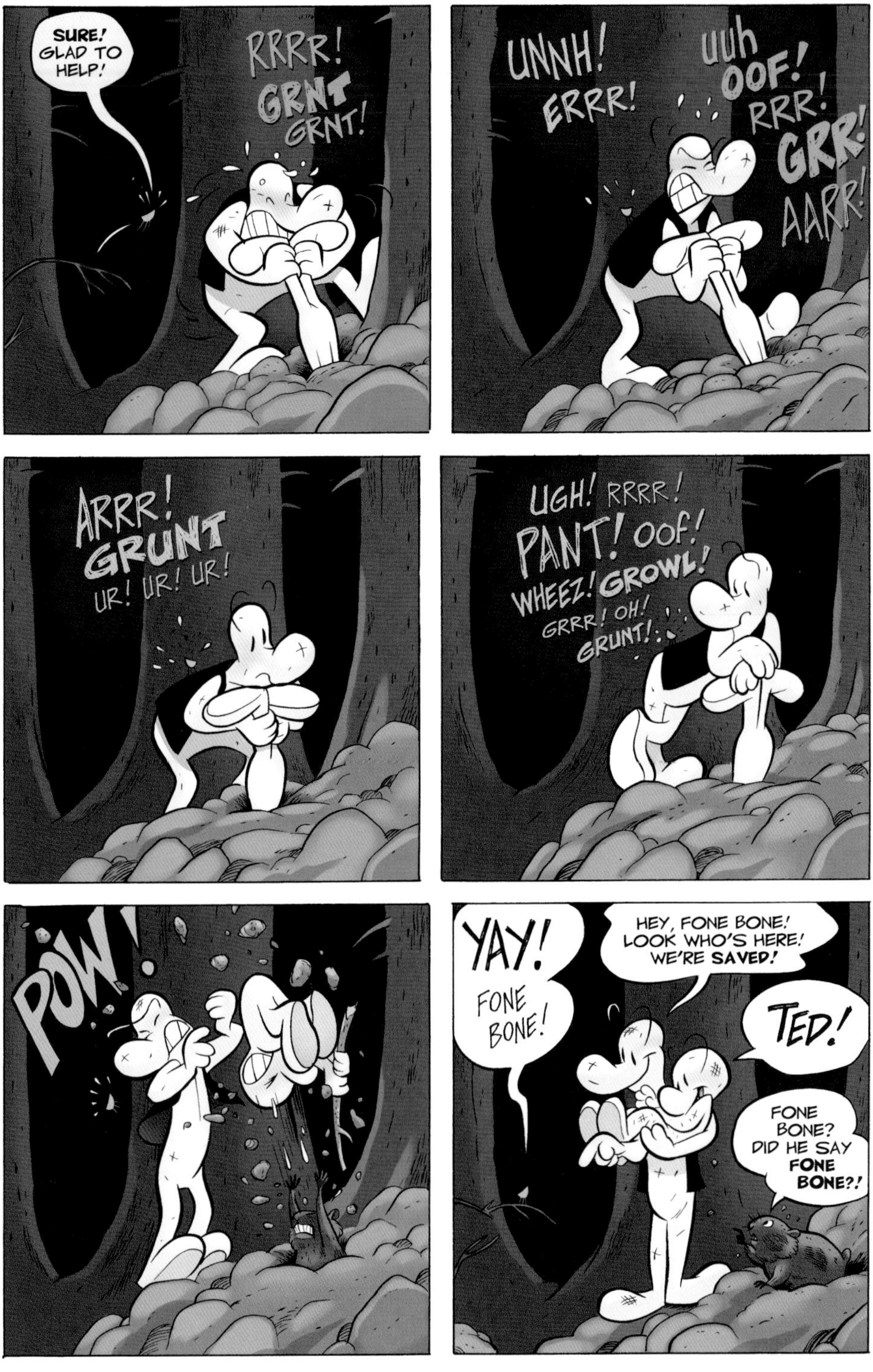
SURE! GLAD TO HELP!
RRRR! GRNT GRNT!
UNNH! ERRR!
uuh OOF! RRR! GRR! AARR!
ARRR! GRUNT UR! UR! UR!
UGH! RRRR! PANT! OOF! WHEEZ! GROWL! GRRR! OH! GRUNT!
POW!
YAY! FONE BONE!
HEY, FONE BONE! LOOK WHO'S HERE! WE'RE SAVED!
TED!
FONE BONE? DID HE SAY FONE BONE?!

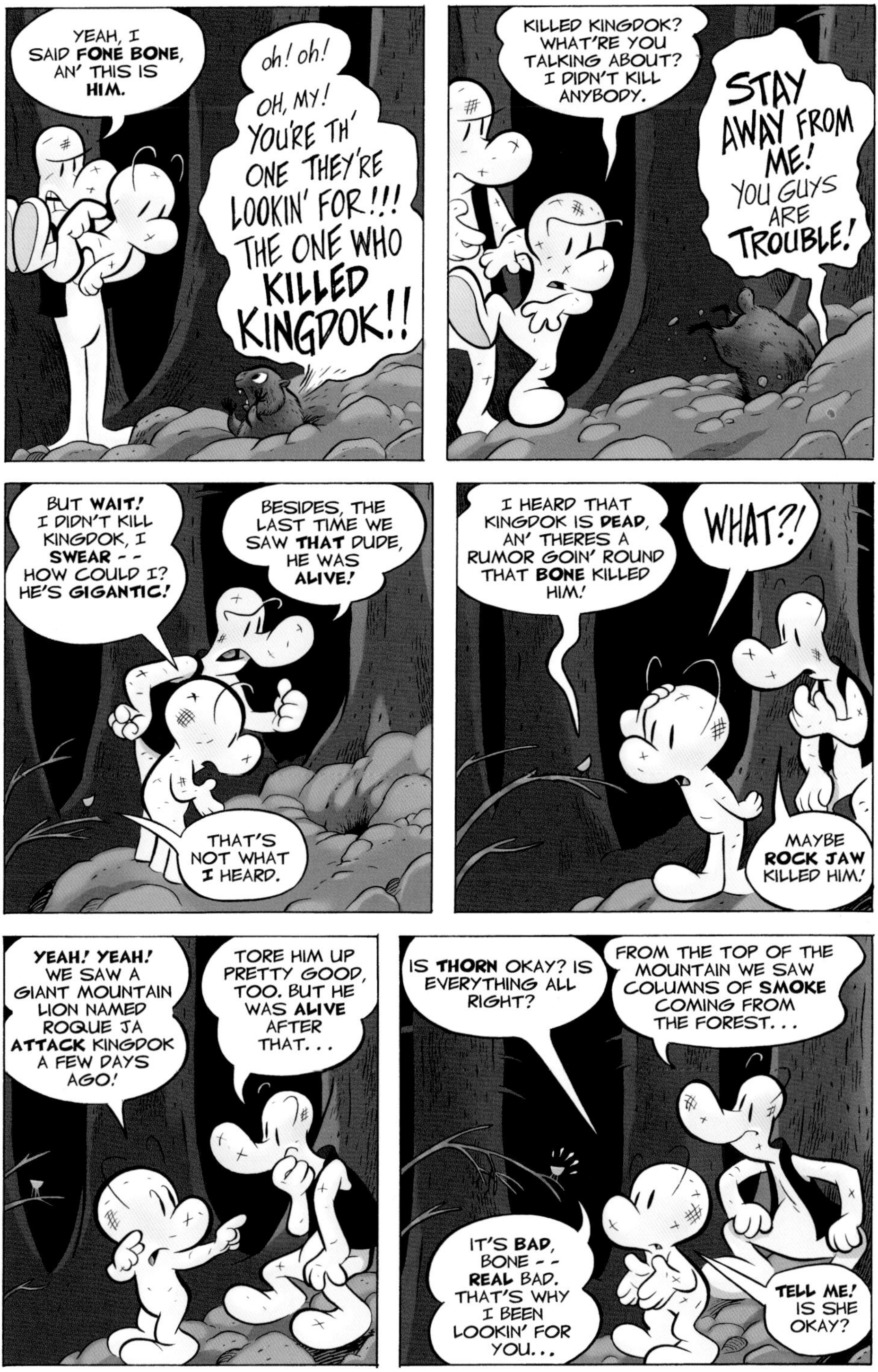
YEAH, I SAID FONE BONE, AN' THIS IS HIM.
oh! oh!
OH, MY! YOU'RE TH' ONE THEY'RE LOOKIN' FOR!!! THE ONE WHO KILLED KINGDOK!!
KILLED KINGDOK? WHAT'RE YOU TALKING ABOUT? I DIDN'T KILL ANYBODY.
STAY AWAY FROM ME! YOU GUYS ARE TROUBLE!
BUT WAIT! I DIDN'T KILL KINGDOK, I SWEAR -- HOW COULD I? HE'S GIGANTIC!
BESIDES, THE LAST TIME WE SAW THAT DUDE, HE WAS ALIVE!
THAT'S NOT WHAT I HEARD.
I HEARD THAT KINGDOK IS DEAD, AN' THERES A RUMOR GOIN' ROUND THAT BONE KILLED HIM!
WHAT?!
MAYBE ROCK JAW KILLED HIM!
YEAH! YEAH! WE SAW A GIANT MOUNTAIN LION NAMED ROQUE JA ATTACK KINGDOK A FEW DAYS AGO!
TORE HIM UP PRETTY GOOD, TOO. BUT HE WAS ALIVE AFTER THAT...
IS THORN OKAY? IS EVERYTHING ALL RIGHT?
FROM THE TOP OF THE MOUNTAIN WE SAW COLUMNS OF SMOKE COMING FROM THE FOREST...
IT'S BAD, BONE -- REAL BAD. THAT'S WHY I BEEN LOOKIN' FOR YOU...
TELL ME! IS SHE OKAY?

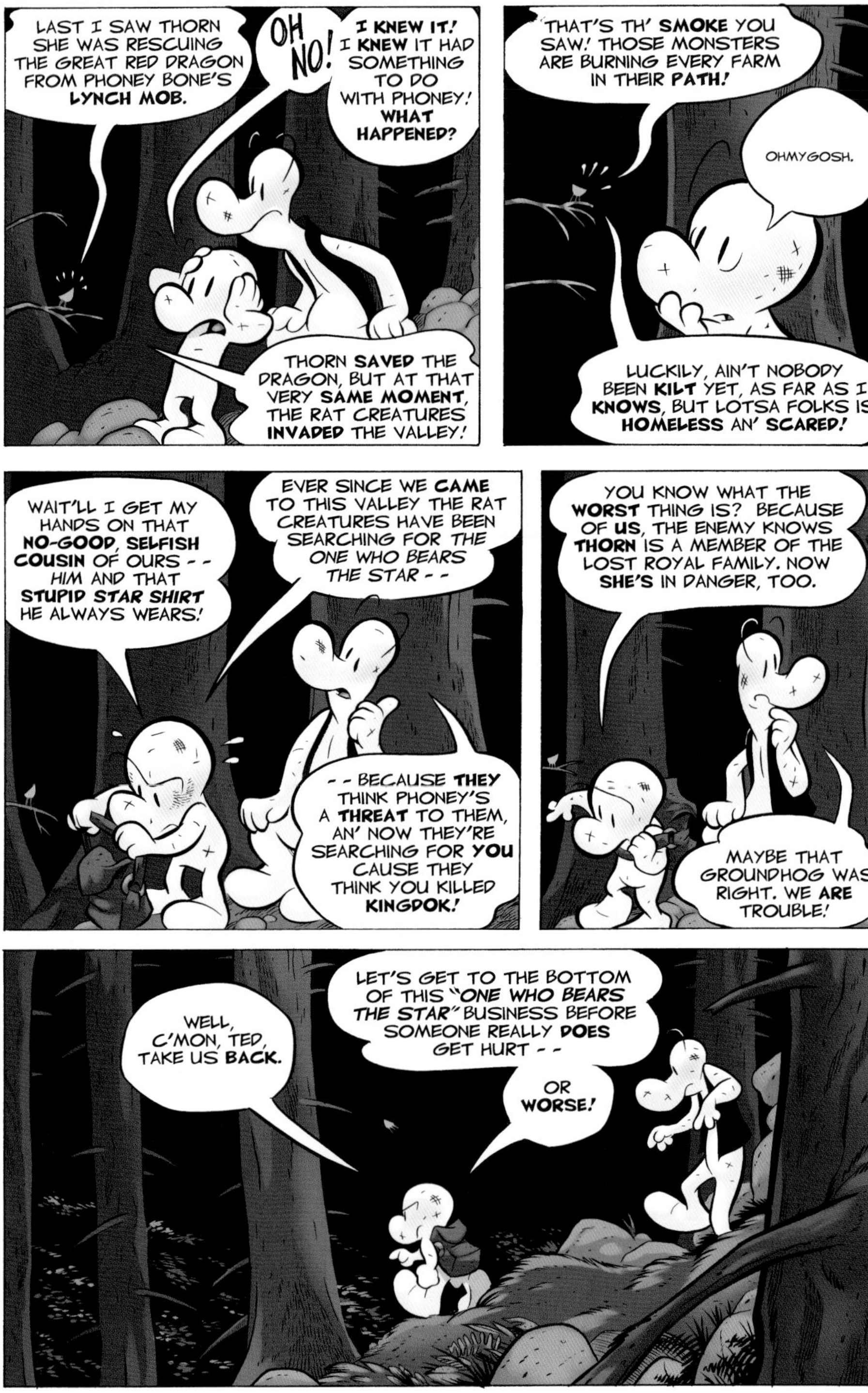
LAST I SAW THORN SHE WAS RESCUING THE GREAT RED DRAGON FROM PHONEY BONE'S **LYNCH MOB.**
OH NO!
I KNEW IT! I **KNEW** IT HAD SOMETHING TO DO WITH PHONEY! **WHAT HAPPENED?**
THORN **SAVED** THE DRAGON, BUT AT THAT VERY **SAME MOMENT**, THE RAT CREATURES **INVADED** THE VALLEY!
THAT'S TH' **SMOKE** YOU SAW! THOSE MONSTERS ARE BURNING EVERY FARM IN THEIR **PATH!**
OHMYGOSH.
LUCKILY, AIN'T NOBODY BEEN **KILT** YET, AS FAR AS I **KNOWS**, BUT LOTSA FOLKS IS **HOMELESS** AN' **SCARED!**
WAIT'LL I GET MY HANDS ON THAT **NO-GOOD, SELFISH COUSIN** OF OURS - - HIM AND THAT **STUPID STAR SHIRT** HE ALWAYS WEARS!
EVER SINCE WE **CAME** TO THIS VALLEY THE RAT CREATURES HAVE BEEN SEARCHING FOR *THE ONE WHO BEARS THE STAR* - -
- - BECAUSE **THEY** THINK PHONEY'S A **THREAT** TO THEM, AN' NOW THEY'RE SEARCHING FOR **YOU** CAUSE THEY THINK YOU KILLED **KINGDOK!**
YOU KNOW WHAT THE **WORST** THING IS? BECAUSE OF **US**, THE ENEMY KNOWS **THORN** IS A MEMBER OF THE LOST ROYAL FAMILY. NOW **SHE'S** IN DANGER, TOO.
MAYBE THAT GROUNDHOG WAS RIGHT. WE **ARE** TROUBLE!
WELL, C'MON, TED, TAKE US **BACK.**
LET'S GET TO THE BOTTOM OF THIS ***"ONE WHO BEARS THE STAR"*** BUSINESS BEFORE SOMEONE REALLY **DOES** GET HURT - -
OR **WORSE!**

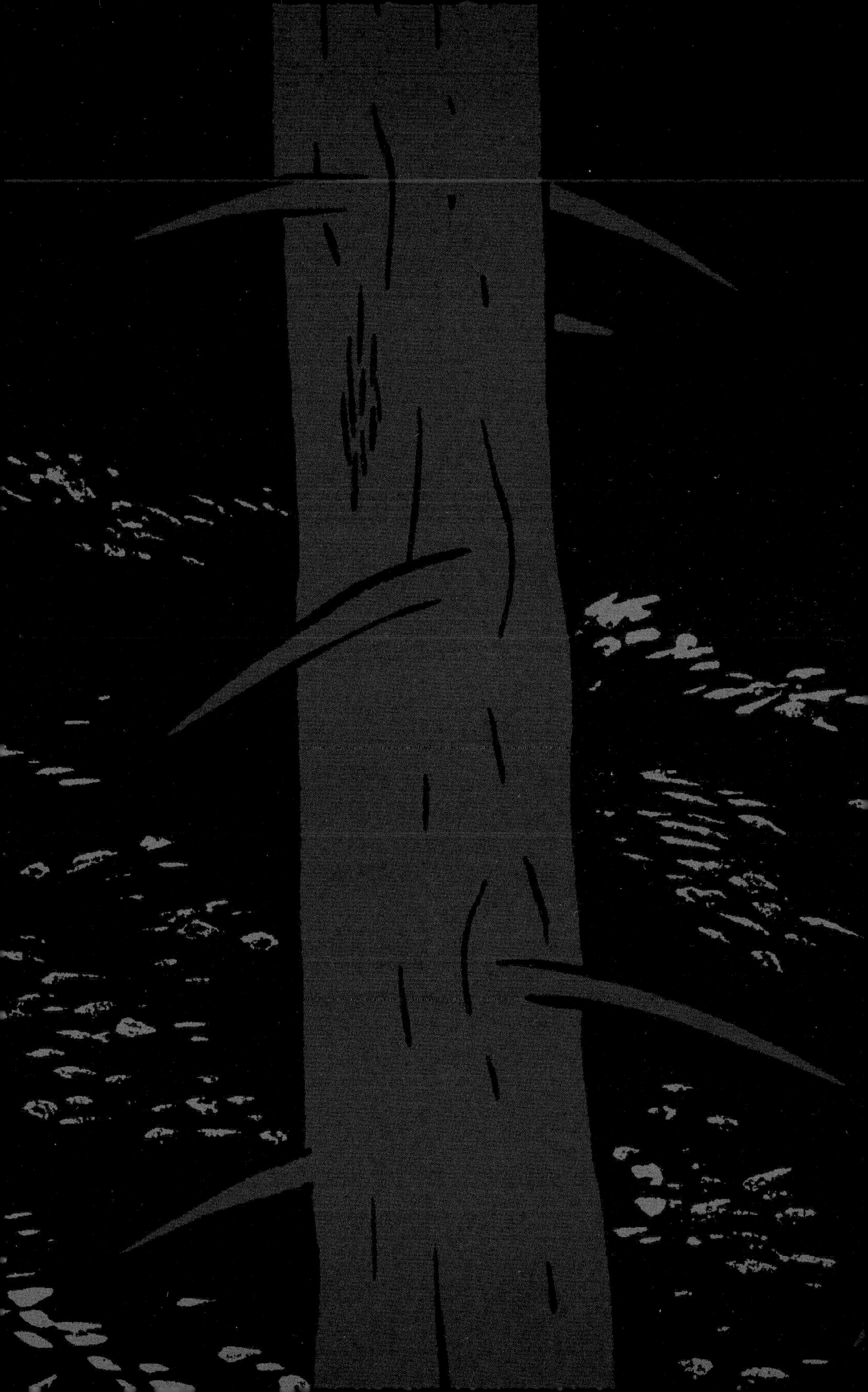

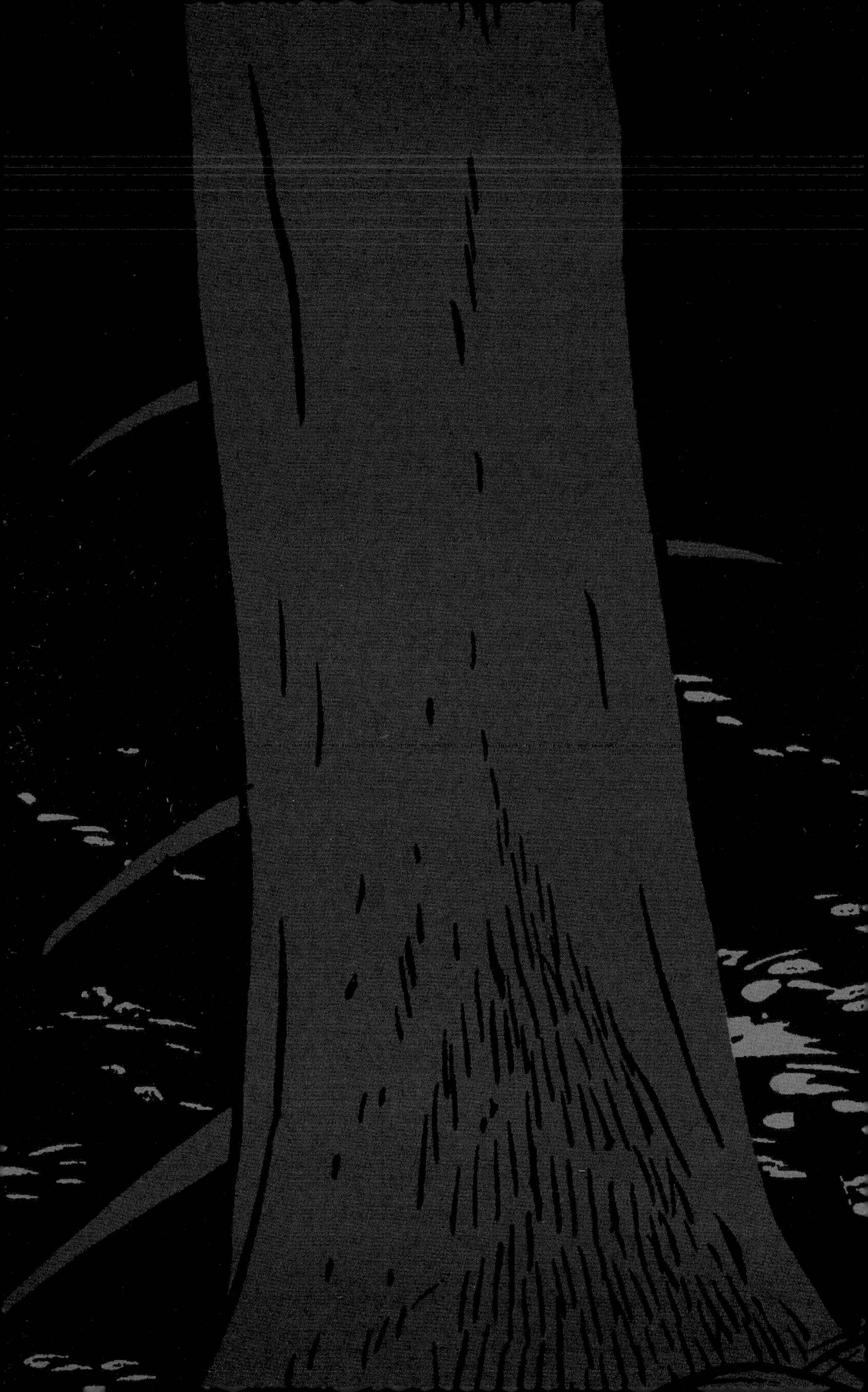

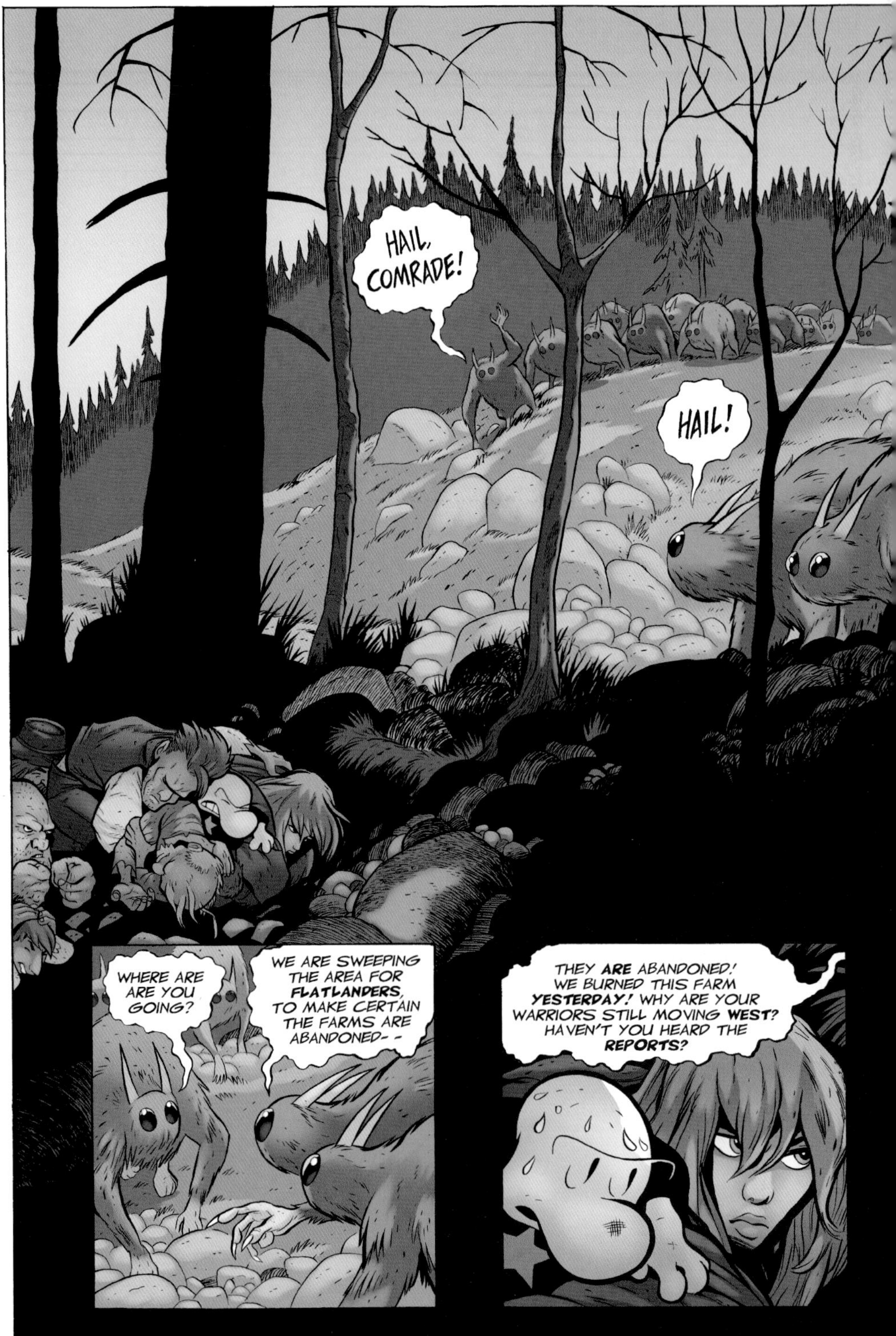
HAIL, COMRADE!
HAIL!
WHERE ARE ARE YOU GOING?
WE ARE SWEEPING THE AREA FOR FLATLANDERS, TO MAKE CERTAIN THE FARMS ARE ABANDONED- -
THEY ARE ABANDONED! WE BURNED THIS FARM YESTERDAY! WHY ARE YOUR WARRIORS STILL MOVING WEST? HAVEN'T YOU HEARD THE REPORTS?

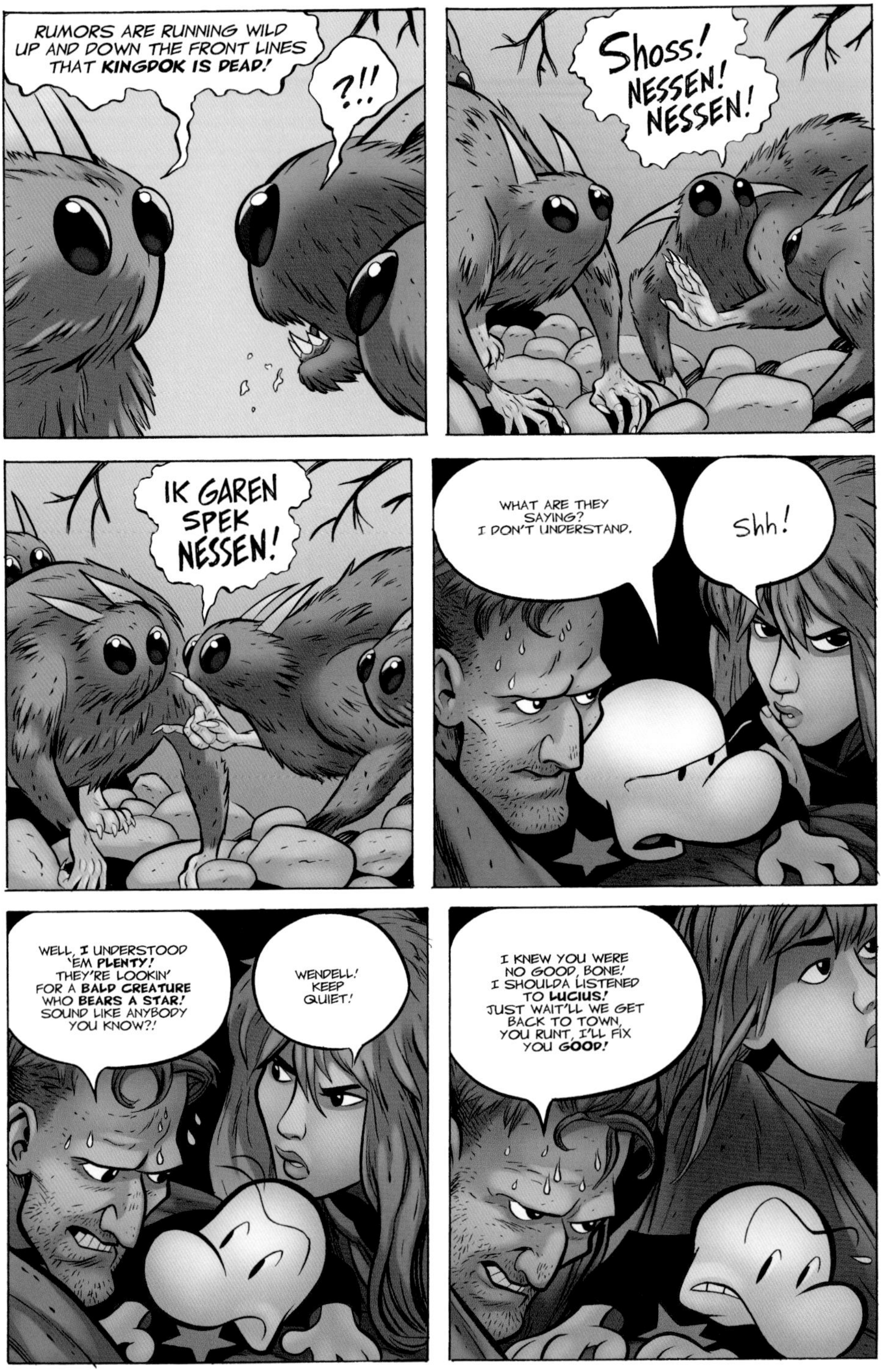
RUMORS ARE RUNNING WILD UP AND DOWN THE FRONT LINES THAT KINGDOK IS DEAD!
?!!
Shoss! NESSEN! NESSEN!
IK GAREN SPEK NESSEN!
WHAT ARE THEY SAYING? I DON'T UNDERSTAND.
Shh!
WELL, I UNDERSTOOD 'EM PLENTY! THEY'RE LOOKIN' FOR A BALD CREATURE WHO BEARS A STAR! SOUND LIKE ANYBODY YOU KNOW?!
WENDELL! KEEP QUIET!
I KNEW YOU WERE NO GOOD, BONE! I SHOULDA LISTENED TO LUCIUS! JUST WAIT'LL WE GET BACK TO TOWN, YOU RUNT, I'LL FIX YOU GOOD!

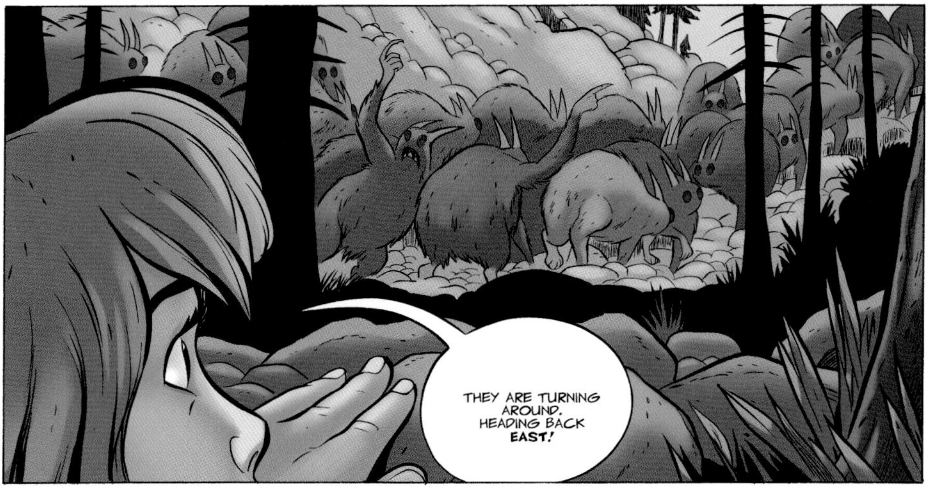
THEY ARE TURNING AROUND. HEADING BACK **EAST!**

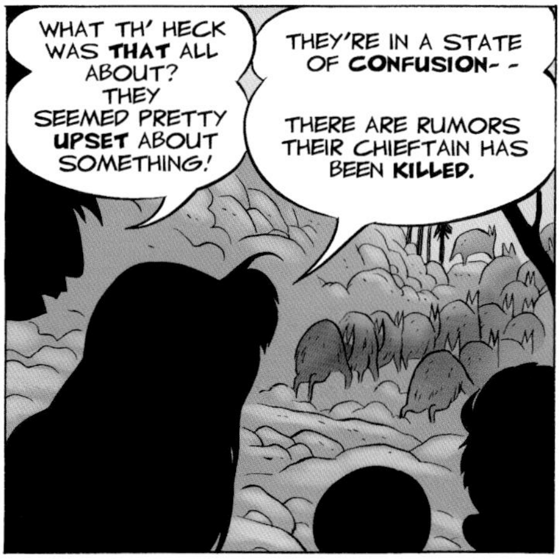
WHAT TH' HECK WAS **THAT** ALL ABOUT? THEY SEEMED PRETTY **UPSET** ABOUT SOMETHING!
THEY'RE IN A STATE OF **CONFUSION**- -
THERE ARE RUMORS THEIR CHIEFTAIN HAS BEEN **KILLED.**

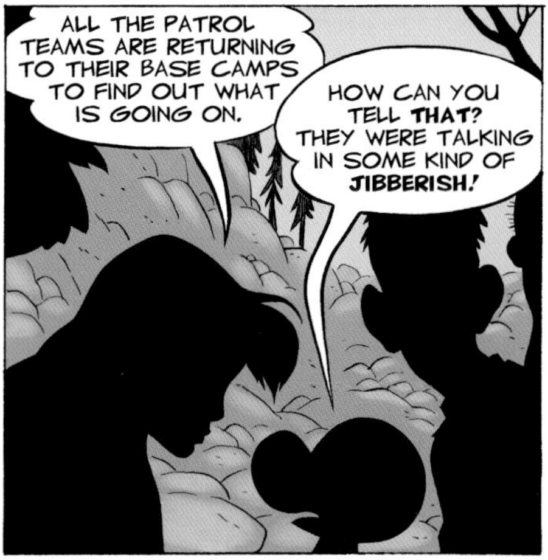
ALL THE PATROL TEAMS ARE RETURNING TO THEIR BASE CAMPS TO FIND OUT WHAT IS GOING ON.
HOW CAN YOU TELL **THAT?** THEY WERE TALKING IN SOME KIND OF **JIBBERISH!**

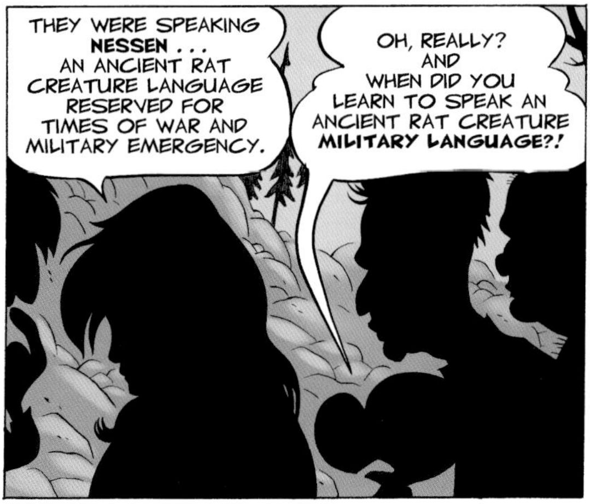
THEY WERE SPEAKING **NESSEN . . .** AN ANCIENT RAT CREATURE LANGUAGE RESERVED FOR TIMES OF WAR AND MILITARY EMERGENCY.
OH, REALLY? AND WHEN DID YOU LEARN TO SPEAK AN ANCIENT RAT CREATURE **MILITARY LANGUAGE?!**

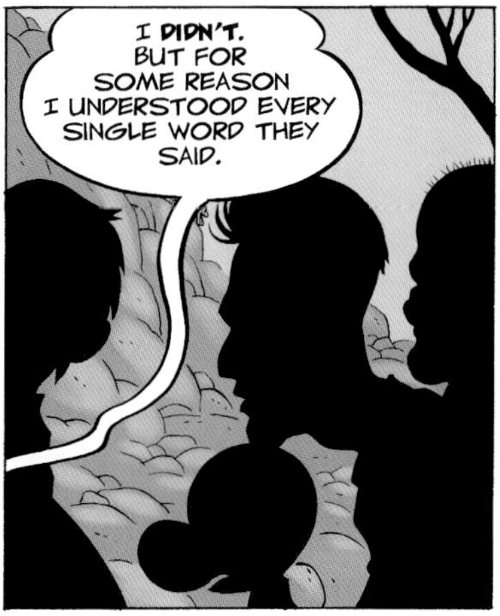
I **DIDN'T.** BUT FOR SOME REASON I UNDERSTOOD EVERY SINGLE WORD THEY SAID.

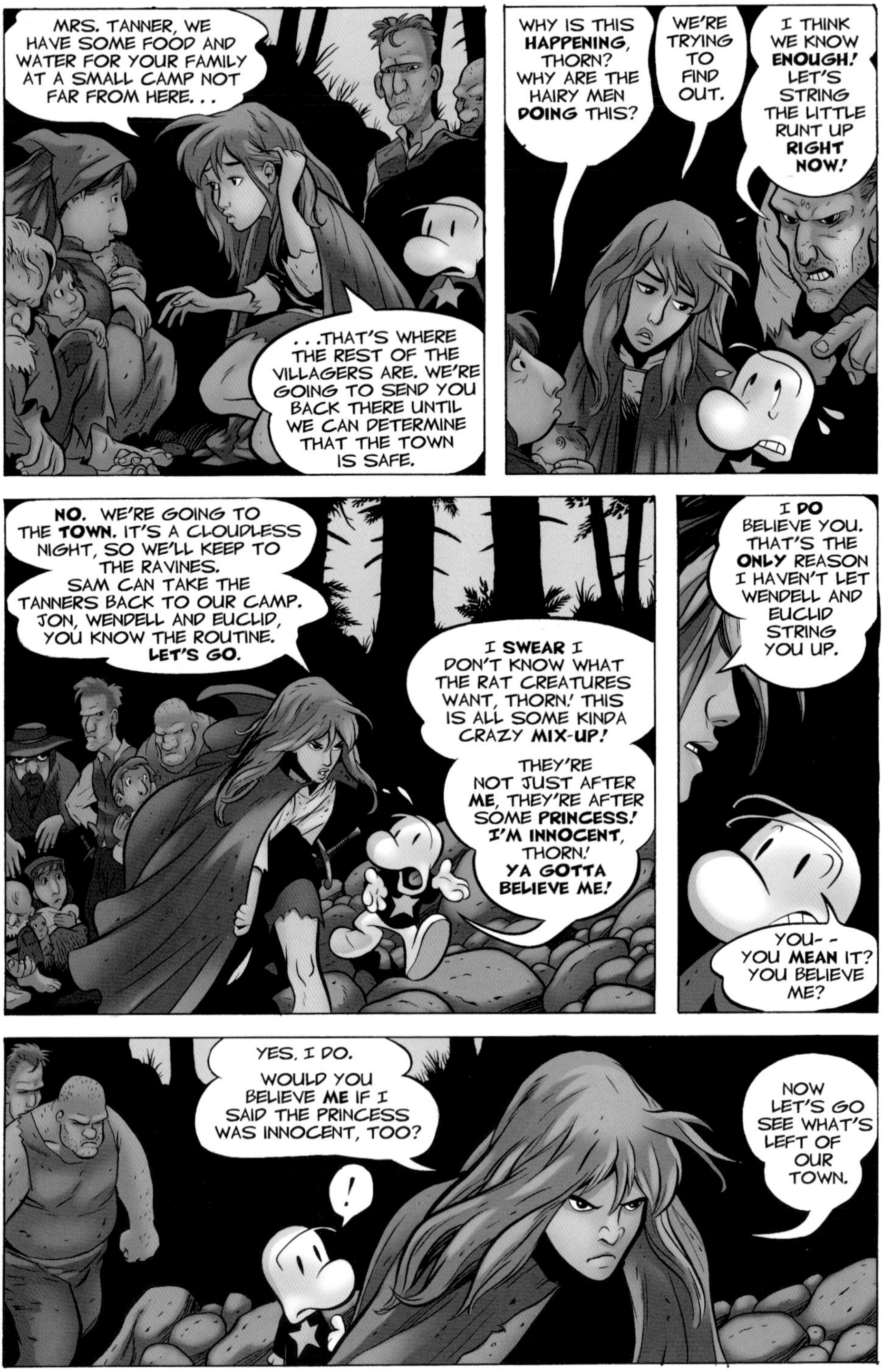
MRS. TANNER, WE HAVE SOME FOOD AND WATER FOR YOUR FAMILY AT A SMALL CAMP NOT FAR FROM HERE. . .
. . .THAT'S WHERE THE REST OF THE VILLAGERS ARE. WE'RE GOING TO SEND YOU BACK THERE UNTIL WE CAN DETERMINE THAT THE TOWN IS SAFE.
WHY IS THIS **HAPPENING**, THORN? WHY ARE THE HAIRY MEN **DOING** THIS?
WE'RE TRYING TO FIND OUT.
I THINK WE KNOW **ENOUGH!** LET'S STRING THE LITTLE RUNT UP **RIGHT NOW!**
NO. WE'RE GOING TO THE **TOWN.** IT'S A CLOUDLESS NIGHT, SO WE'LL KEEP TO THE RAVINES. SAM CAN TAKE THE TANNERS BACK TO OUR CAMP. JON, WENDELL AND EUCLID, YOU KNOW THE ROUTINE. **LET'S GO.**
I **SWEAR** I DON'T KNOW WHAT THE RAT CREATURES WANT, THORN! THIS IS ALL SOME KINDA CRAZY **MIX-UP!**
THEY'RE NOT JUST AFTER **ME**, THEY'RE AFTER SOME **PRINCESS! I'M INNOCENT**, THORN! **YA GOTTA BELIEVE ME!**
I **DO** BELIEVE YOU. THAT'S THE **ONLY** REASON I HAVEN'T LET WENDELL AND EUCLID STRING YOU UP.
YOU- - YOU **MEAN** IT? YOU BELIEVE ME?
YES, I DO.
WOULD YOU BELIEVE **ME** IF I SAID THE PRINCESS WAS INNOCENT, TOO?
!
NOW LET'S GO SEE WHAT'S LEFT OF OUR TOWN.

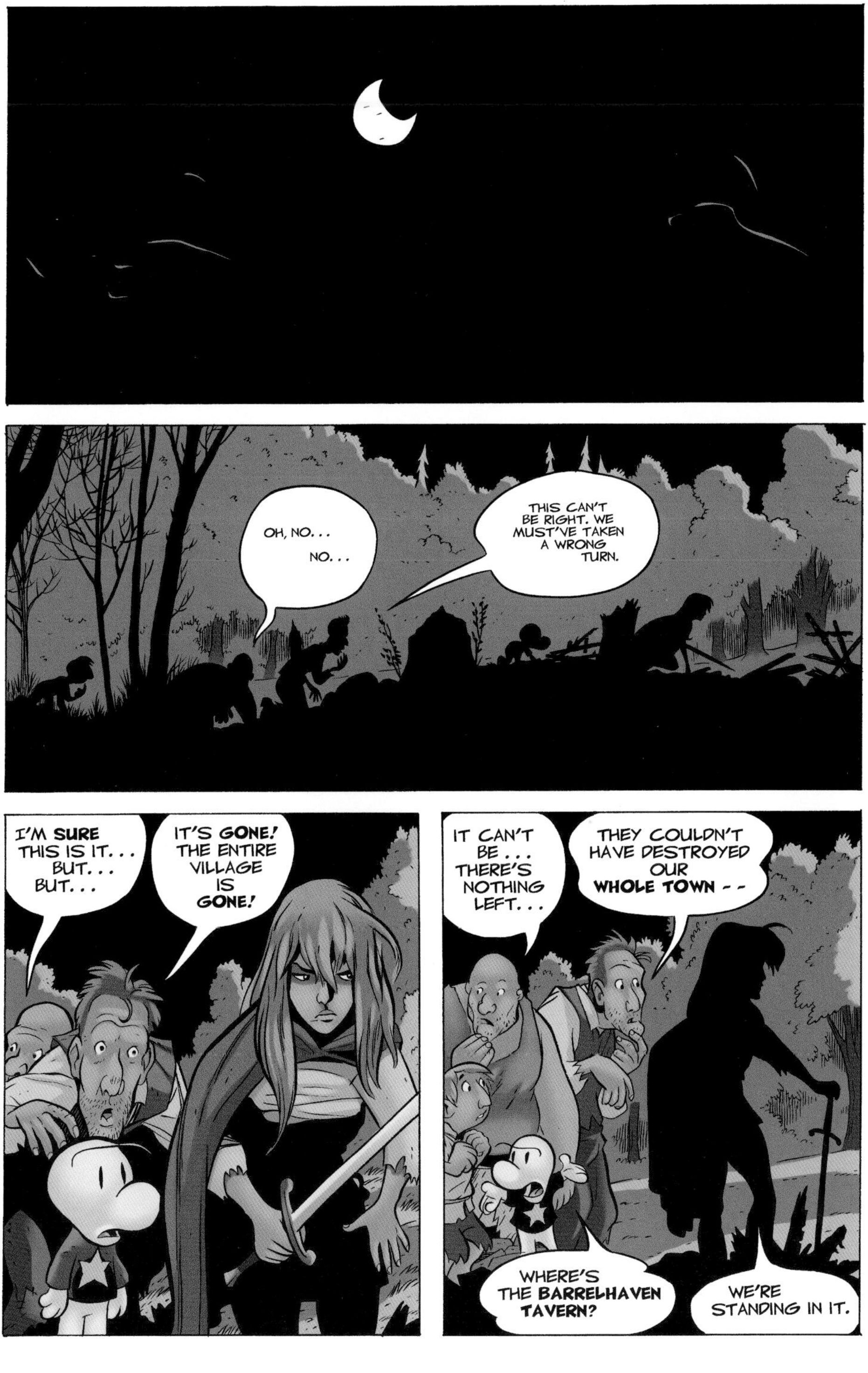
OH, NO. . .
NO. . .
THIS CAN'T BE RIGHT. WE MUST'VE TAKEN A WRONG TURN.
I'M **SURE** THIS IS IT. . . BUT. . . BUT. . .
IT'S **GONE!** THE ENTIRE VILLAGE IS **GONE!**
IT CAN'T BE . . . THERE'S NOTHING LEFT. . .
THEY COULDN'T HAVE DESTROYED OUR **WHOLE TOWN** - -
WHERE'S THE **BARRELHAVEN TAVERN?**
WE'RE STANDING IN IT.

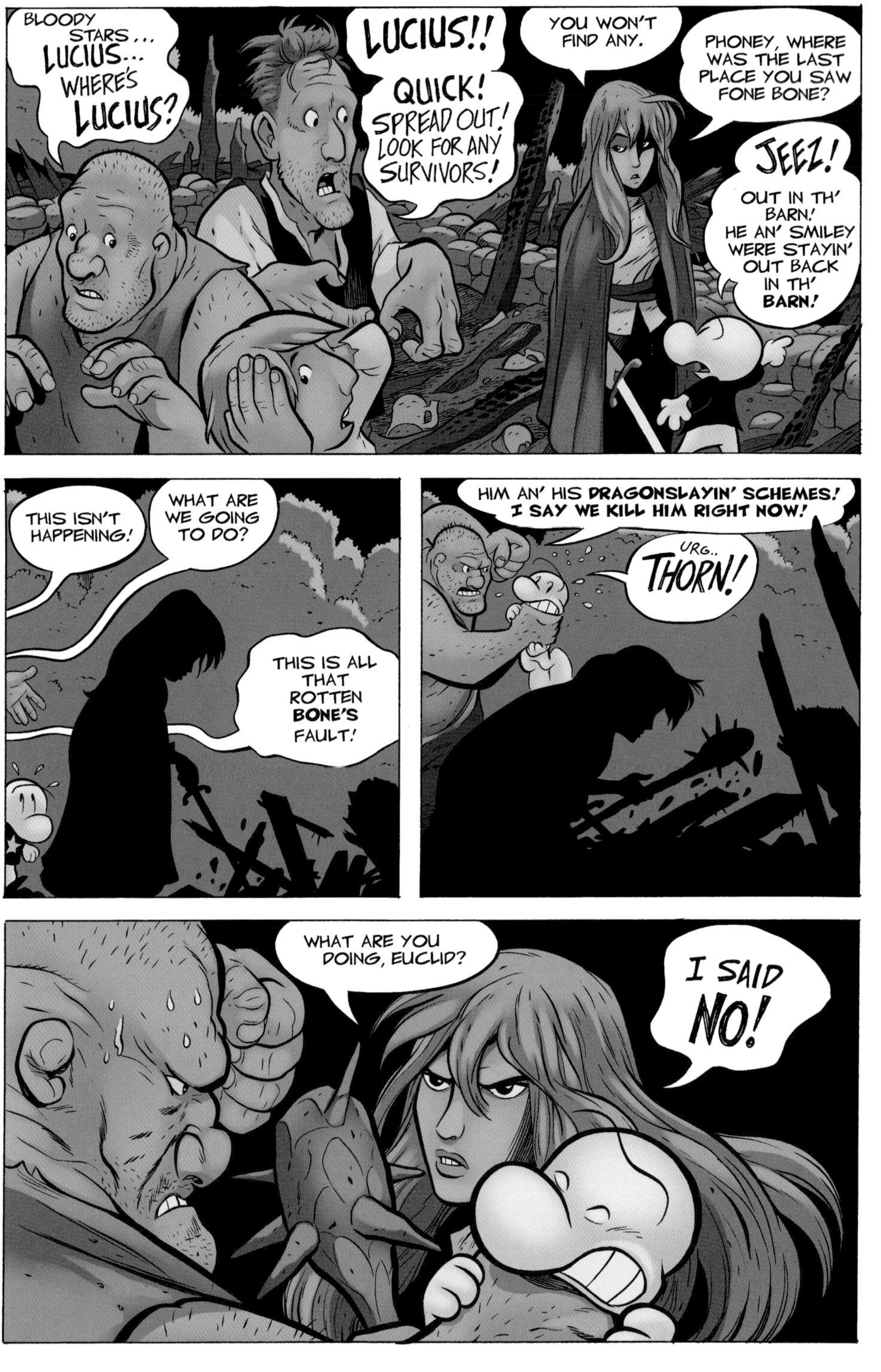
BLOODY STARS... LUCIUS... WHERE'S LUCIUS?
LUCIUS!!
QUICK! SPREAD OUT! LOOK FOR ANY SURVIVORS!
YOU WON'T FIND ANY.
PHONEY, WHERE WAS THE LAST PLACE YOU SAW FONE BONE?
JEEZ!
OUT IN TH' BARN! HE AN' SMILEY WERE STAYIN' OUT BACK IN TH' **BARN!**
THIS ISN'T HAPPENING!
WHAT ARE WE GOING TO DO?
THIS IS ALL THAT ROTTEN **BONE'S** FAULT!
HIM AN' HIS **DRAGONSLAYIN' SCHEMES! I SAY WE KILL HIM RIGHT NOW!**
URG..
THORN!
WHAT ARE YOU DOING, EUCLID?
I SAID NO!

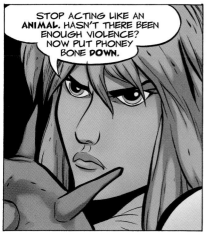

STOP ACTING LIKE AN **ANIMAL.** HASN'T THERE BEEN ENOUGH VIOLENCE? NOW PUT PHONEY BONE **DOWN.**

NO!! HE SWINDLED US AND **DESTROYED** OUR TOWN!

HE DIDN'T ATTACK THE VILLAGE! THE **RAT CREATURES** DID!

HE TRICKED US INTO CHASIN' AFTER **DRAGONS!** WE WERE AWAY FROM OUR **HOMES** WHEN WE SHOULDA BEEN **HERE** DEFENDING THE **VILLAGE!**

NOBODY **FORCED** YOU TO FOLLOW HIM! YOU WERE A **MOB** LOOKING FOR SCAPEGOATS!

BUT IF WE HAD BEEN **HERE,** THEN LUCIUS MIGHT STILL BE **ALIVE!**

WE DON'T KNOW WHAT HAPPENED TO LUCIUS... BUT WHATEVER IT WAS, IF YOU **HAD** BEEN HERE, YOU WOULD HAVE **SHARED** HIS FATE!

AND SO WOULD ALL THE OTHER VILLAGERS WHO WERE **WITH** YOU HUNTING DRAGONS! THIS BONE PROBABLY SAVED **HALF THE VILLAGE** BY TAKING YOU UP INTO THE MOUNTAINS!

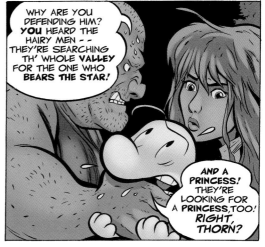

WHY ARE YOU DEFENDING HIM? **YOU** HEARD THE HAIRY MEN -- THEY'RE SEARCHING TH' WHOLE **VALLEY** FOR THE ONE WHO **BEARS THE STAR!**

AND A **PRINCESS!** THEY'RE LOOKING FOR A **PRINCESS, TOO!** RIGHT, THORN?

SHUT UP, YOU!

SCRINCH

GURK!

KEEP IT UP, EUCLID! THE MORE WE BEHAVE LIKE **BRUTES**, THE MORE POWER OUR **ENEMIES** HAVE!

WHAT DO **YOU** SAY, WENDELL? DO WE **STRING HIM UP** OR **NOT**?

I DON'T KNOW...

GIK GURK

...THIS MUCH DESTRUCTION

MAYBE THORN'S **RIGHT**. THERE'S BEEN **ENOUGH** VIOLENCE.

YOU DON'T WANNA LET HIM **OFF THE HOOK**, DO YA?

GERK!

WE'RE AS MUCH TO BLAME AS HE IS! GET **AHOLD OF YOURSELF!**

I'LL GET HOLD OF MYSELF RIGHT AFTER I **TWIST HIS SCRAWNY NECK!**

IT'S THORN!! IT'S **THORN!** SHE'S TH' **PRINCESS!!**

GO ON, YER MAJESTY, **ORDER THIS APE OFF** OF ME!

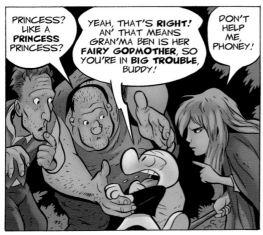

PRINCESS? LIKE A **PRINCESS** PRINCESS?

YEAH, THAT'S **RIGHT!** AN' THAT MEANS GRAN'MA BEN IS HER **FAIRY GODMOTHER**, SO YOU'RE IN **BIG TROUBLE**, BUDDY!

DON'T HELP ME, PHONEY!

THE RAT CREATURES **WERE** SEARCHING FOR A PRINCESS...

OKAY, OKAY, THE RAT CREATURES **MAY** THINK I'M A PRINCESS, **THAT** MUCH IS TRUE.

A **PRINCESS**? **HOW**? FROM **WHERE**?! THE ROYAL FAMILY WAS KILLED IN THE BIG **WAR**!

THERE HASN'T BEEN A KINGDOM FOR ALMOST **FIFTEEN YEARS**!

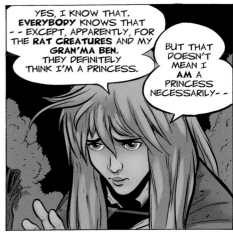

YES, I KNOW THAT. **EVERYBODY** KNOWS THAT - - EXCEPT, APPARENTLY, FOR THE **RAT CREATURES** AND MY **GRAN'MA BEN**. THEY DEFINITELY THINK I'M A PRINCESS.

BUT THAT DOESN'T MEAN I **AM** A PRINCESS NECESSARILY- -

SHE DOES KINDA **LOOK** LIKE A PRINCESS.

YES, BUT WHAT DOES THAT MAKE OL' **ROSE BEN**? THE LOST QUEEN OF THE **VALLEY**? OL' GRAN'MA BEN RACES **COWS**, REMEMBER. . .

LOOK, I DON'T KNOW IF IT'S TRUE. . . BUT I **AM** SURE WE SHOULDN'T BE DISCUSSING IT **HERE**!

THAT MEANS **YOU** CAN JUST KEEP YOUR **TRAP SHUT** - - UNDERSTAND?

YEAH, YEAH. WE ALL GOT OUR LITTLE **DELUSIONS OF GRANDEUR**. I COULD TELL YOU WANTED TO GET IT OFF YOUR CHEST.

LISTEN UP. THIS WAR CLUB BELONGS TO MY FRIEND **FONE BONE**. I FOUND IT HERE IN THE WRECKAGE OF THE BARN, AND THERE'S A GOOD CHANCE HE AND SOME OTHERS **ESCAPED**. . .

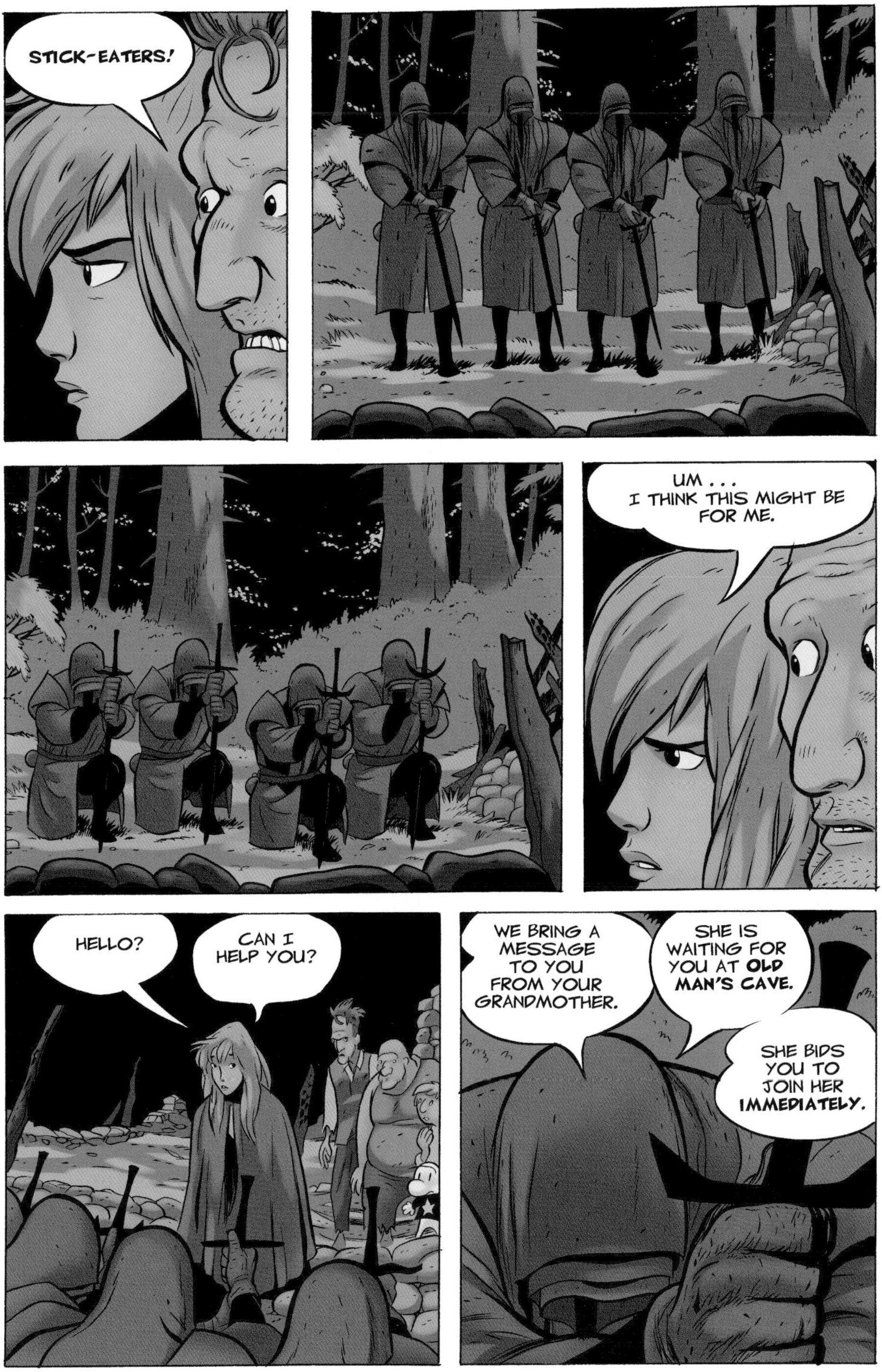
STICK-EATERS!
UM . . . I THINK THIS MIGHT BE FOR ME.
HELLO?
CAN I HELP YOU?
WE BRING A MESSAGE TO YOU FROM YOUR GRANDMOTHER.
SHE IS WAITING FOR YOU AT OLD MAN'S CAVE.
SHE BIDS YOU TO JOIN HER IMMEDIATELY.

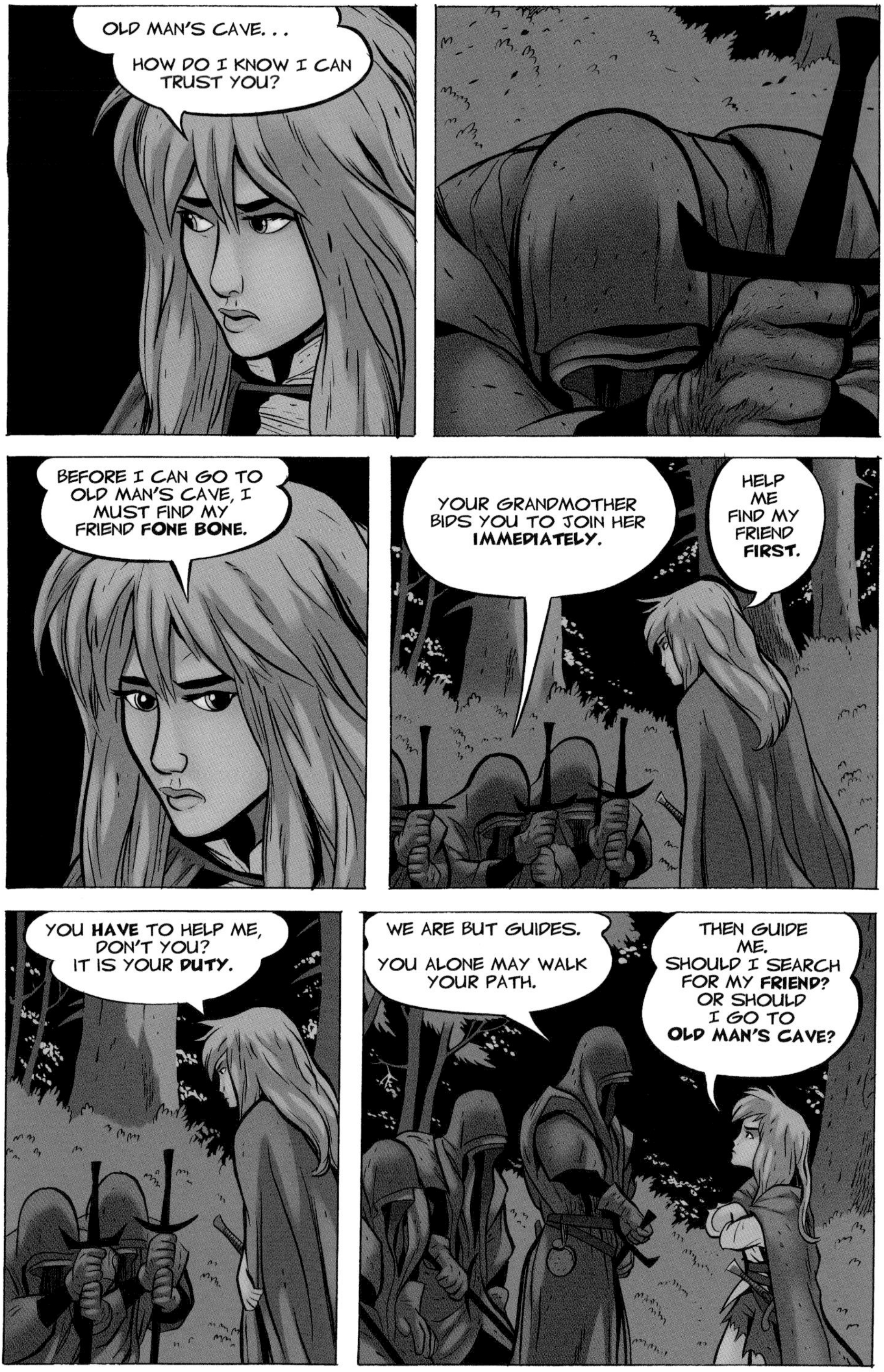
OLD MAN'S CAVE. . .
HOW DO I KNOW I CAN TRUST YOU?
BEFORE I CAN GO TO OLD MAN'S CAVE, I MUST FIND MY FRIEND **FONE BONE.**
YOUR GRANDMOTHER BIDS YOU TO JOIN HER **IMMEDIATELY.**
HELP ME FIND MY FRIEND **FIRST.**
YOU **HAVE** TO HELP ME, DON'T YOU? IT IS YOUR **DUTY.**
WE ARE BUT GUIDES.
YOU ALONE MAY WALK YOUR PATH.
THEN GUIDE ME. SHOULD I SEARCH FOR MY **FRIEND?** OR SHOULD I GO TO **OLD MAN'S CAVE?**

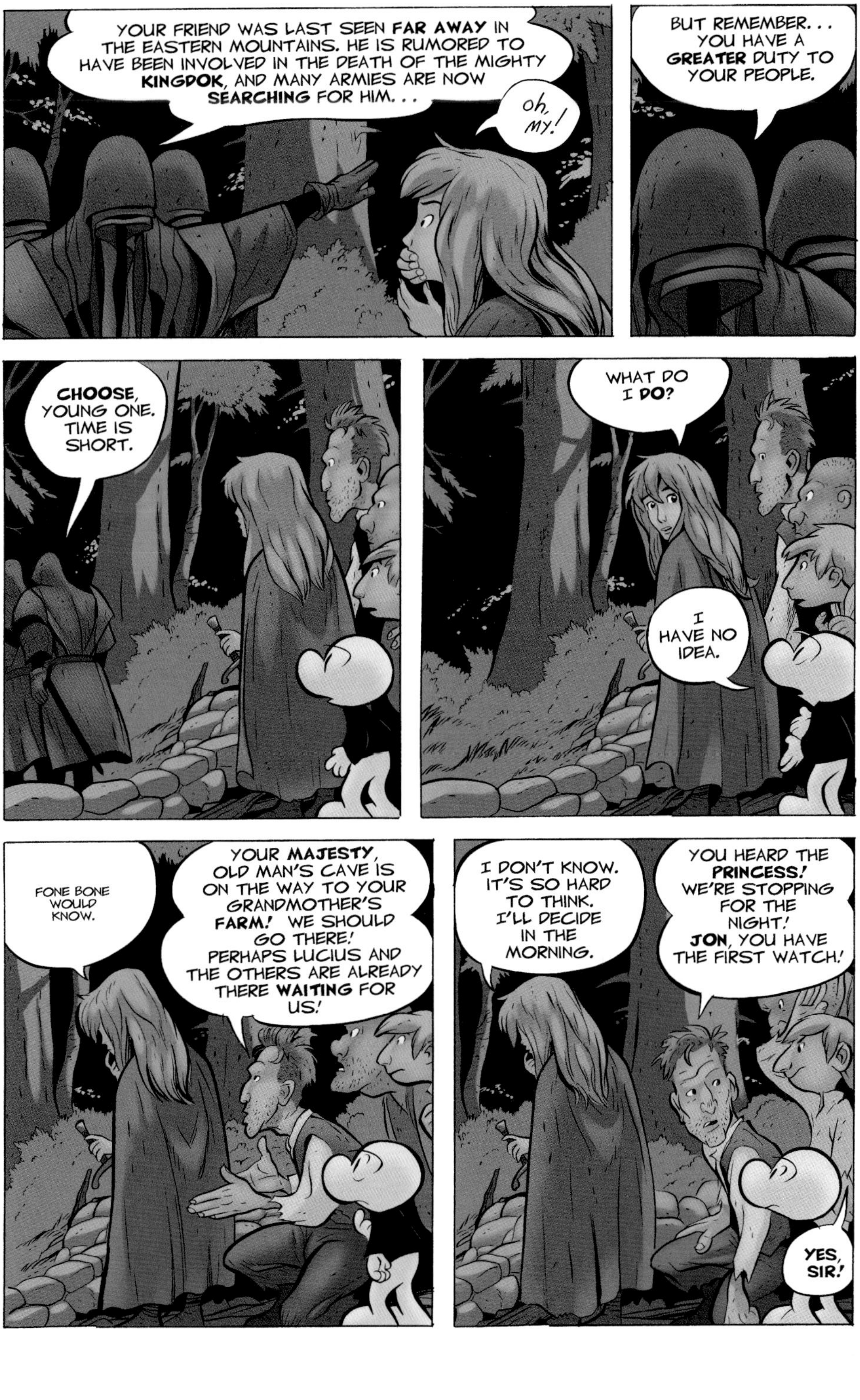
YOUR FRIEND WAS LAST SEEN FAR AWAY IN THE EASTERN MOUNTAINS. HE IS RUMORED TO HAVE BEEN INVOLVED IN THE DEATH OF THE MIGHTY KINGDOK, AND MANY ARMIES ARE NOW SEARCHING FOR HIM. . .
oh, my!
BUT REMEMBER. . . YOU HAVE A GREATER DUTY TO YOUR PEOPLE.
CHOOSE, YOUNG ONE. TIME IS SHORT.
WHAT DO I DO?
I HAVE NO IDEA.
FONE BONE WOULD KNOW.
YOUR MAJESTY, OLD MAN'S CAVE IS ON THE WAY TO YOUR GRANDMOTHER'S FARM! WE SHOULD GO THERE! PERHAPS LUCIUS AND THE OTHERS ARE ALREADY THERE WAITING FOR US!
I DON'T KNOW. IT'S SO HARD TO THINK. I'LL DECIDE IN THE MORNING.
YOU HEARD THE PRINCESS! WE'RE STOPPING FOR THE NIGHT! JON, YOU HAVE THE FIRST WATCH!
YES, SIR!

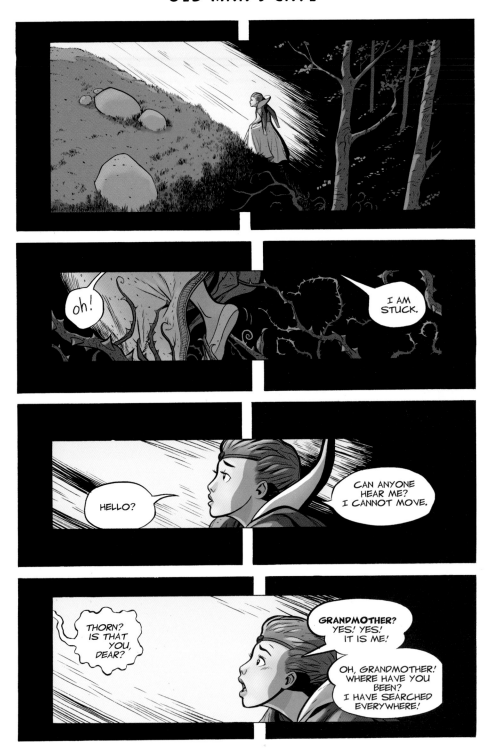

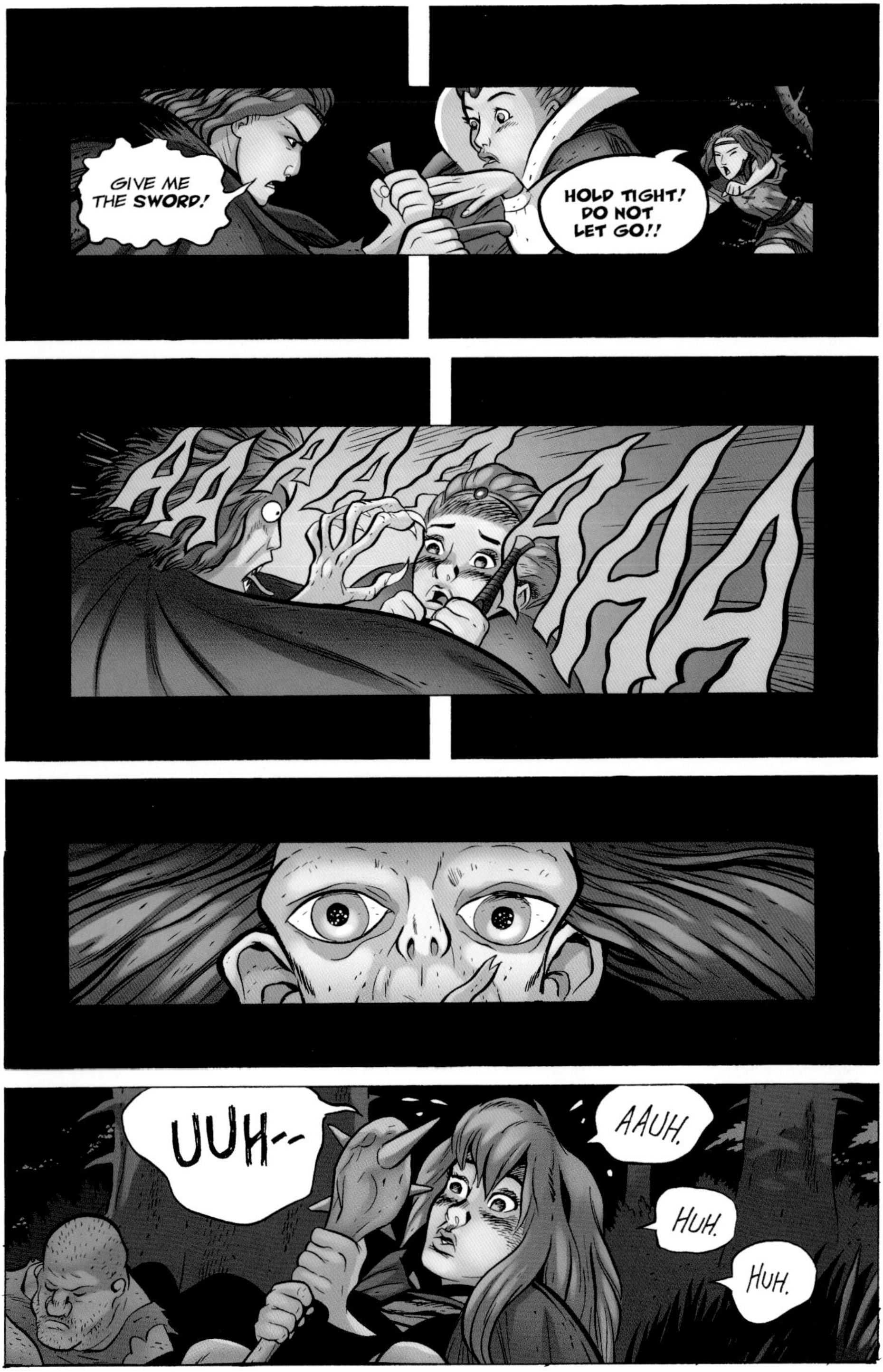
GIVE ME THE **SWORD!**
HOLD TIGHT! DO NOT LET GO!!
UUH--
AAUH.
HUH.
HUH.

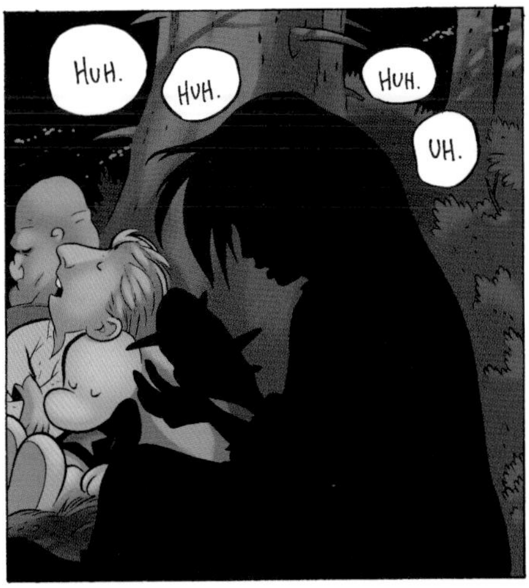
HUH.
HUH.
HUH.
UH.

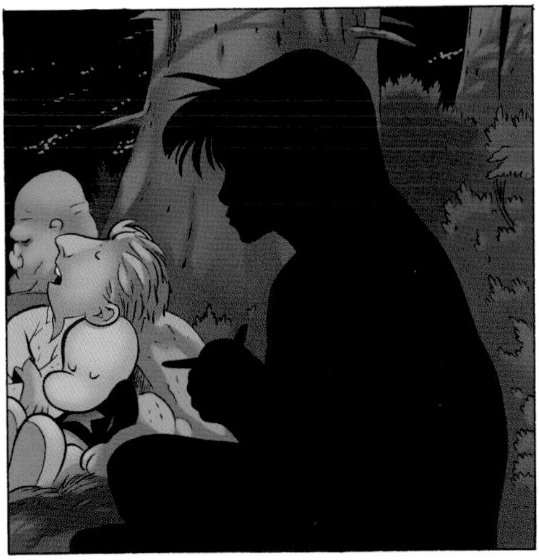

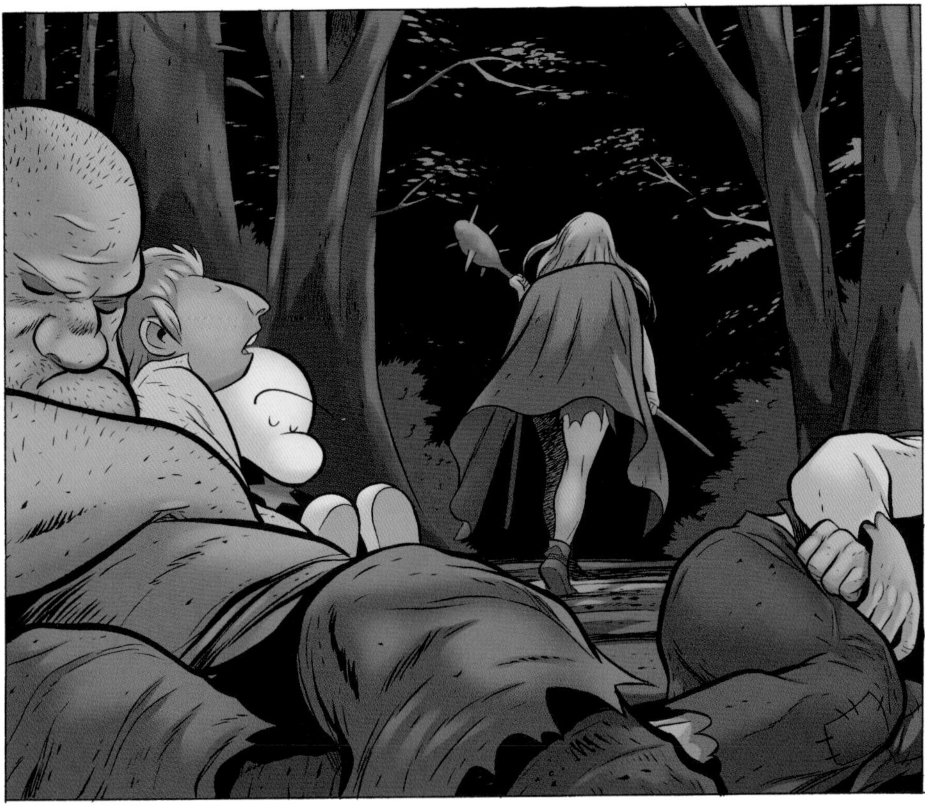

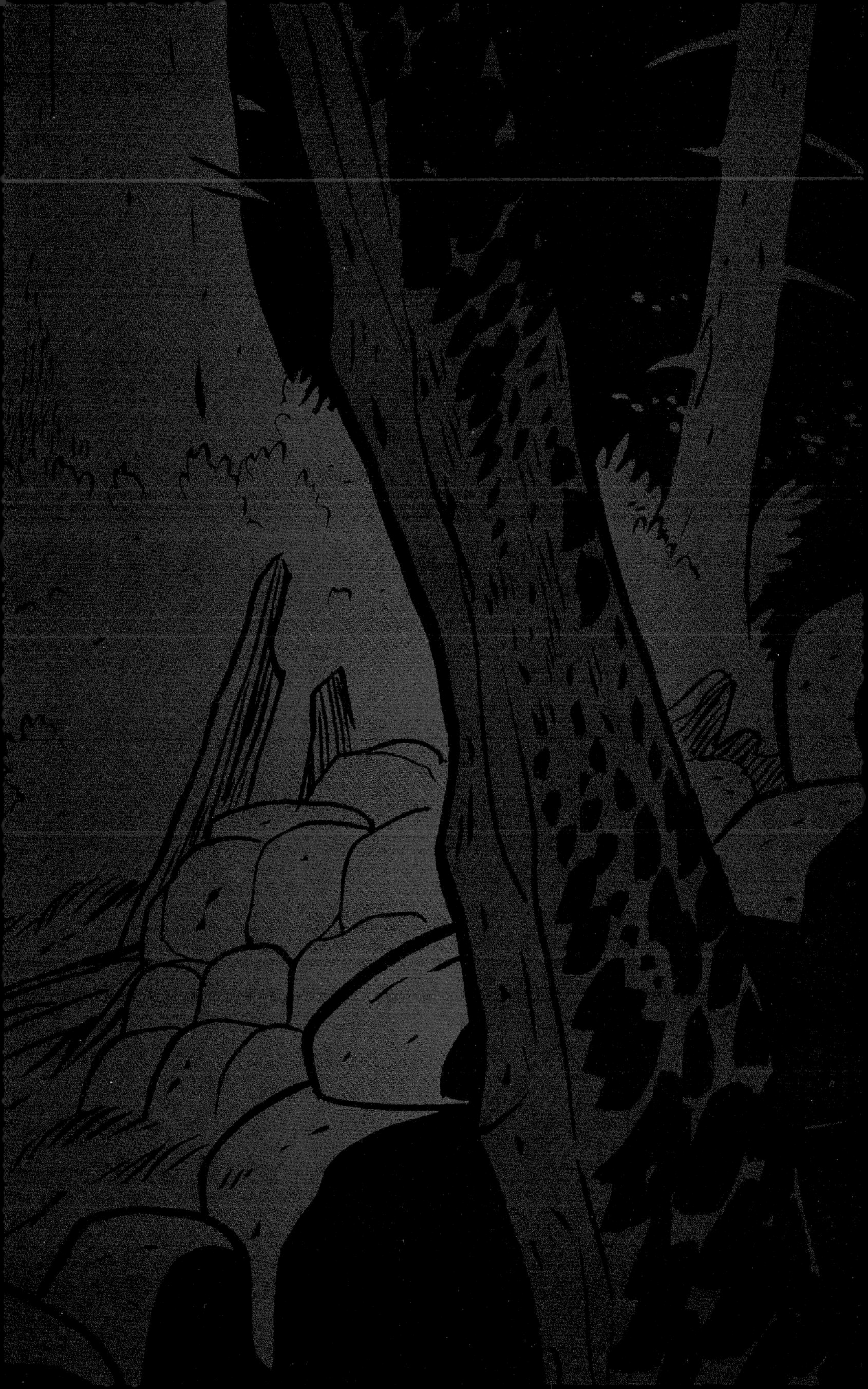

THORN COULD'VE FOUND HER WAY THROUGH THIS RAIN. **SHE COULD** FIND HER WAY IN TH' **DARKEST NIGHT** LIKE SHE WAS FOLLOWING A MAP.

YES, SHE COULD. IT'S **UNCANNY.**

hmmf.

SHE FOLLOWS THE **DRAGONS IN THE EARTH.** JUST LIKE TH' DRAGON TOLD HER.

YEAH, WELL, SHE'S FOLLOWIN' DRAGONS **SOMEWHERE ELSE!** **FORGET HER!** WE GOT PROBLEMS OF OUR OWN– –

HEY!

THAT'S IT.. I'VE **HAD IT!**

SPLOSH!

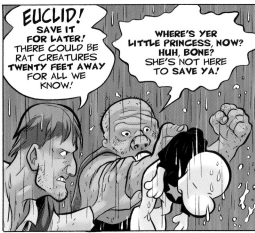

EUCLID! SAVE IT FOR LATER! THERE COULD BE RAT CREATURES **TWENTY FEET AWAY** FOR ALL WE KNOW!

WHERE'S YER **LITTLE PRINCESS, NOW? HUH, BONE?** SHE'S NOT HERE TO SAVE YA!

PUT HIM **DOWN,** EUCLID!

STAY BACK! I'VE **HAD** IT WITH THIS **TROUBLEMAKER!** **THIS IS ALL HIS FAULT!**

ALL RIGHT, THAT'S ENOUGH. I DON'T KNOW WHERE THORN **IS,** BUT UNTIL SHE GETS BACK, I'M **ENFORCING HER ORDERS!**

YOU'RE A **FOOL,** WENDELL! SHE RAN OUT ON US LAST NIGHT! WHAT DO YOU **CARE** WHAT SHE WANTS?!

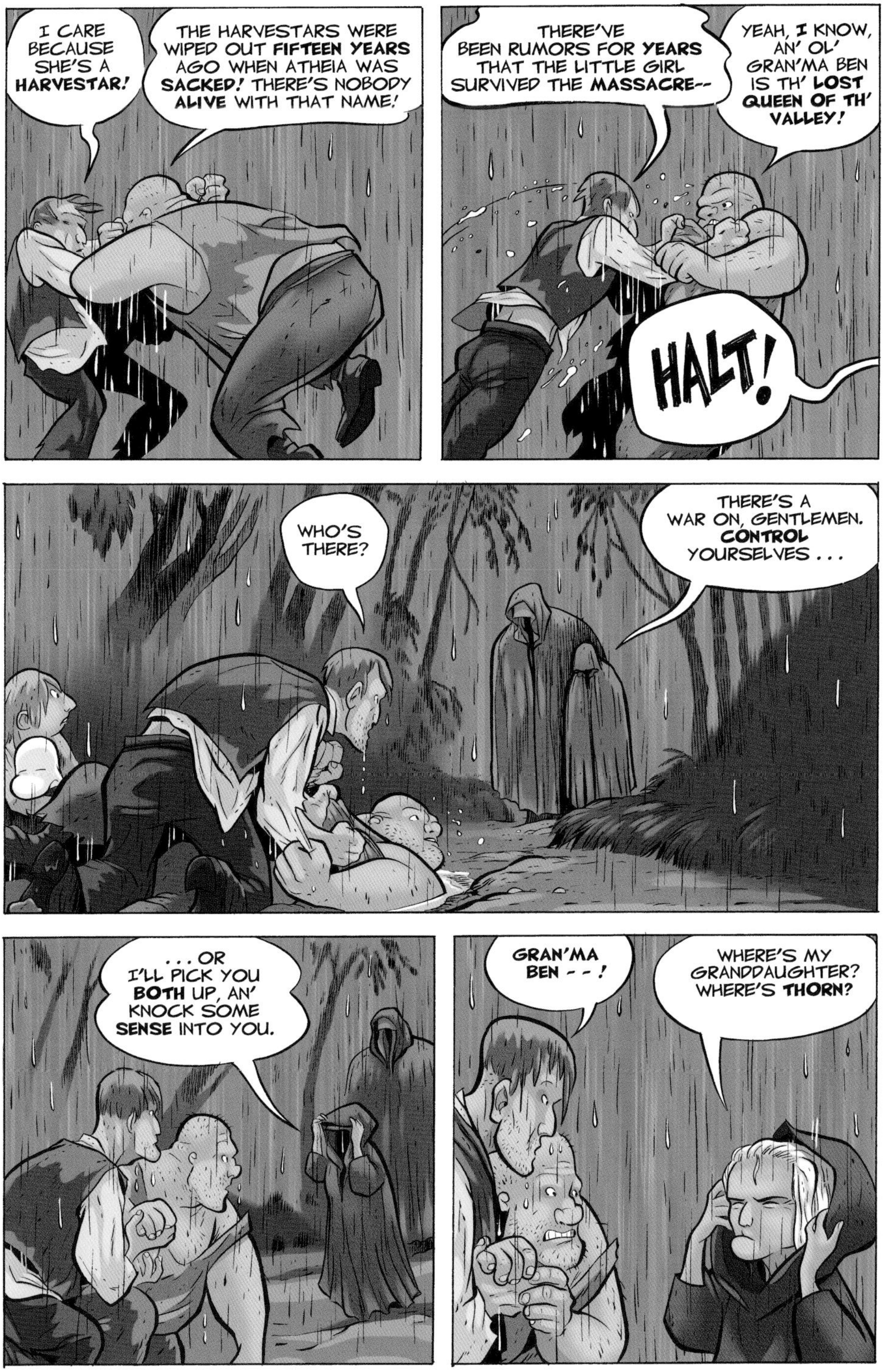
I CARE BECAUSE SHE'S A HARVESTAR!
THE HARVESTARS WERE WIPED OUT FIFTEEN YEARS AGO WHEN ATHEIA WAS SACKED! THERE'S NOBODY ALIVE WITH THAT NAME!
THERE'VE BEEN RUMORS FOR YEARS THAT THE LITTLE GIRL SURVIVED THE MASSACRE--
YEAH, I KNOW, AN' OL' GRAN'MA BEN IS TH' LOST QUEEN OF TH' VALLEY!
HALT!
WHO'S THERE?
THERE'S A WAR ON, GENTLEMEN. CONTROL YOURSELVES . . .
. . . OR I'LL PICK YOU BOTH UP, AN' KNOCK SOME SENSE INTO YOU.
GRAN'MA BEN - - !
WHERE'S MY GRANDDAUGHTER? WHERE'S THORN?

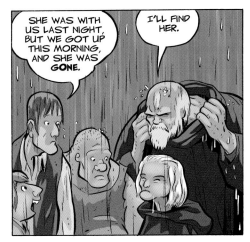

SHE WAS WITH US LAST NIGHT, BUT WE GOT UP THIS MORNING, AND SHE WAS **GONE**.

I'LL FIND HER.

LUCIUS! YOU'RE ALIVE!

COME WITH ME. WE'RE NEAR THE CAVE NOW, AND YOU CAN DRY OFF - -

TH - THAT'S AMAZING.

LUCIUS TOOK OFF AFTER THORN WITHOUT A **SECOND THOUGHT** ABOUT HIS OWN SAFETY.

THAT'S RIGHT. HE'S A VERY REMARKABLE MAN.

I'M SURPRISED YOU NOTICED, PHONCIBLE.

COME. IT'S NOT SAFE OUT HERE, YOU'LL CATCH YOUR **DEATH**.

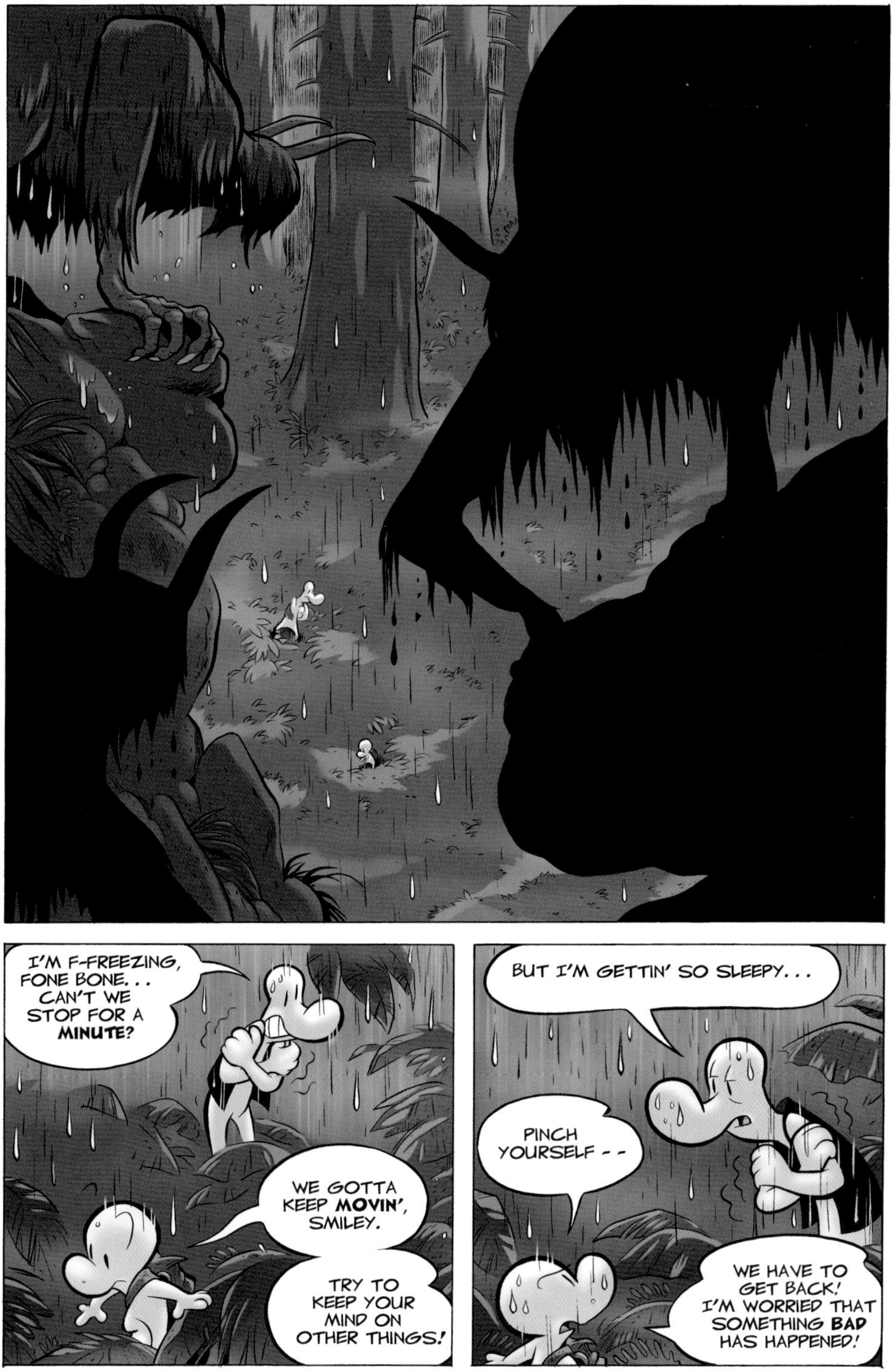
I'M F-FREEZING, FONE BONE. . . CAN'T WE STOP FOR A **MINUTE?**
WE GOTTA KEEP **MOVIN'**, SMILEY.
TRY TO KEEP YOUR MIND ON OTHER THINGS!
BUT I'M GETTIN' SO SLEEPY. . .
PINCH YOURSELF - -
WE HAVE TO GET BACK! I'M WORRIED THAT SOMETHING **BAD** HAS HAPPENED!

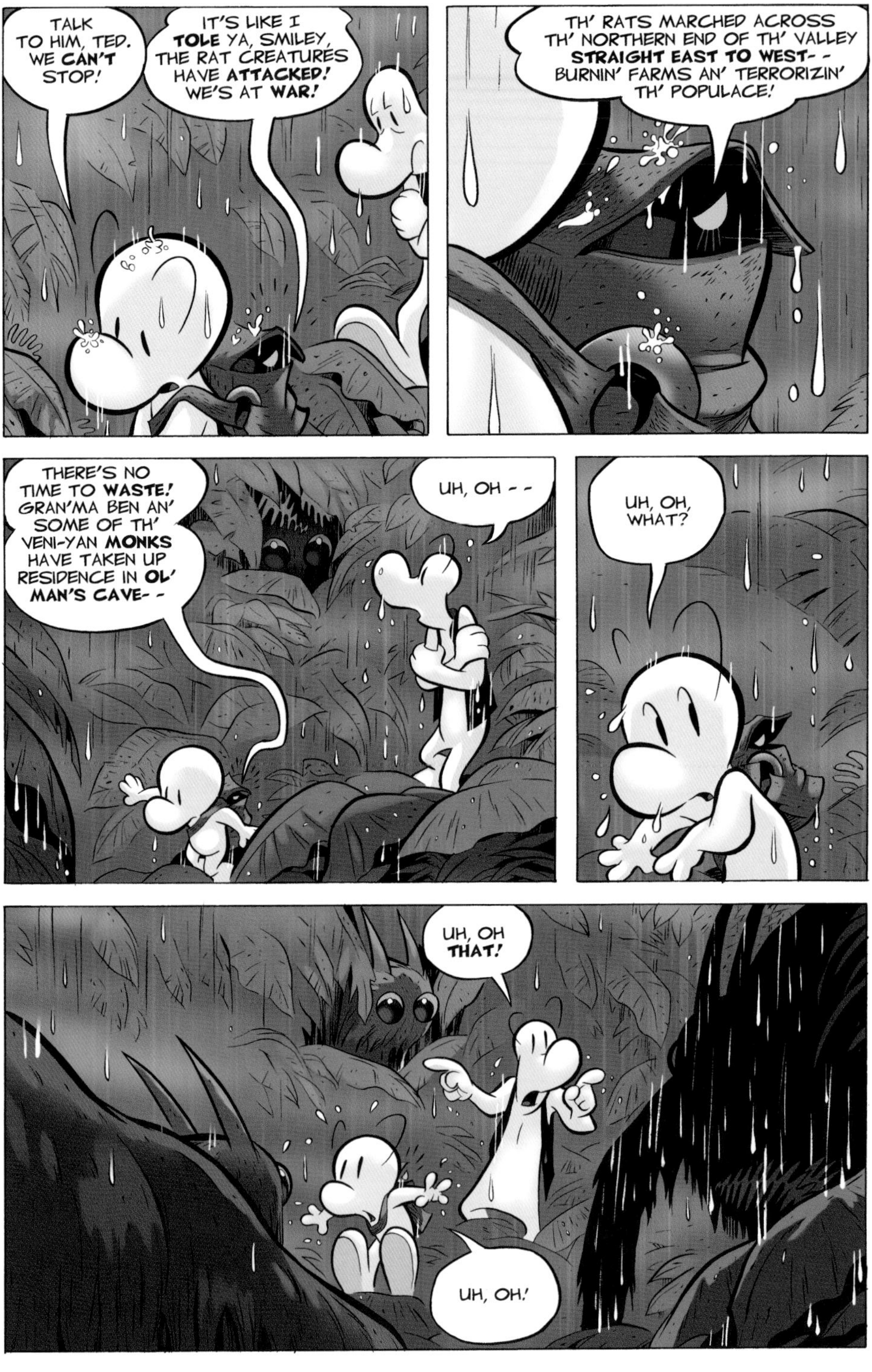
TALK TO HIM, TED. WE CAN'T STOP!
IT'S LIKE I TOLE YA, SMILEY, THE RAT CREATURES HAVE ATTACKED! WE'S AT WAR!
TH' RATS MARCHED ACROSS TH' NORTHERN END OF TH' VALLEY STRAIGHT EAST TO WEST- - BURNIN' FARMS AN' TERRORIZIN' TH' POPULACE!
THERE'S NO TIME TO WASTE! GRAN'MA BEN AN' SOME OF TH' VENI-YAN MONKS HAVE TAKEN UP RESIDENCE IN OL' MAN'S CAVE- -
UH, OH - -
UH, OH, WHAT?
UH, OH THAT!
UH, OH!

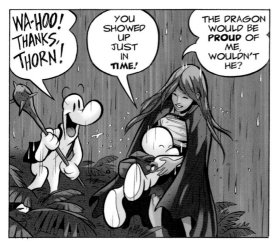

WA-HOO! THANKS, THORN!

YOU SHOWED UP JUST IN **TIME!**

THE DRAGON WOULD BE **PROUD** OF ME, WOULDN'T HE?

I'LL SAY! THAT RESCUE WAS AS **LAST MINUTE** AS ANY THE **DRAGON** EVER MADE -- ANY DAY!

HA HA!

GOSH, IT'S GOOD TO SEE YOU AGAIN.

YOU TOO. AND I'M PROBABLY GOING TO GET IN **BIG TROUBLE** FOR COMING.

HIYA, THORNY! IT'S ME, TED TH' BUG! WHY'S YOU GONNA GET IN **TROUBLE** FOR?

GRAN'MA BEN WANTED ME TO MEET HER AT **OLD MAN'S CAVE.** SHE'S LOOKING FOR ME.

SPEAKING OF WHICH, WE BETTER GET MOVING.

WE'RE KINDA **LOST.** EVEN TED CAN'T TELL WHICH WAY IS WHICH IN THIS **RAIN!**

YEAH, THORNY. WHICH WAY IS OL' MAN'S CAVE FROM HERE?

WELL, LET'S SEE. . .

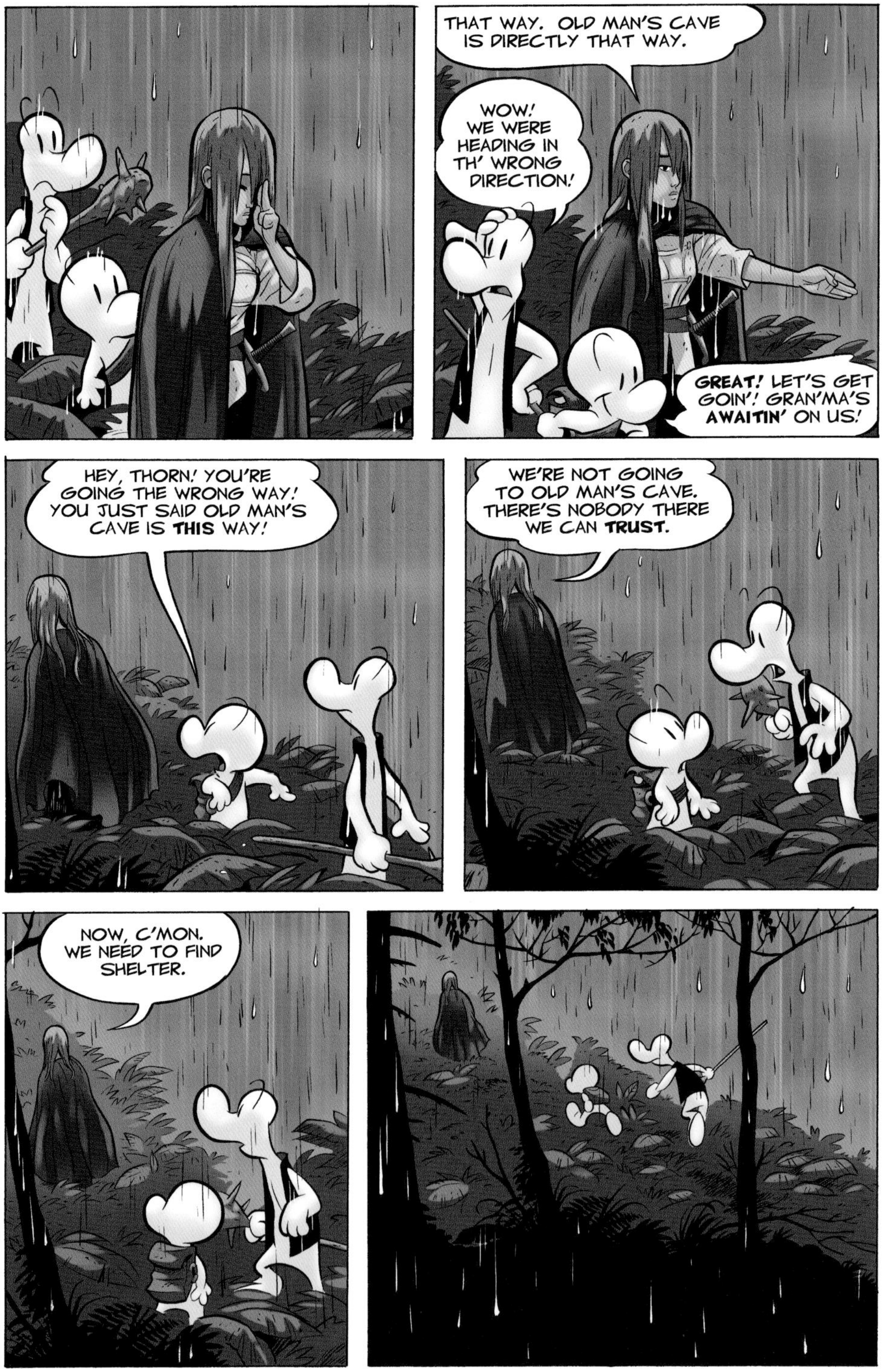
THAT WAY. OLD MAN'S CAVE IS DIRECTLY THAT WAY.
WOW! WE WERE HEADING IN TH' WRONG DIRECTION!
GREAT! LET'S GET GOIN'! GRAN'MA'S **AWAITIN'** ON US!
HEY, THORN! YOU'RE GOING THE WRONG WAY! YOU JUST SAID OLD MAN'S CAVE IS **THIS** WAY!
WE'RE NOT GOING TO OLD MAN'S CAVE. THERE'S NOBODY THERE WE CAN **TRUST**.
NOW, C'MON. WE NEED TO FIND SHELTER.

MASTER . . .
PLEASE DO NOT BE ANGRY . . .
OUR PLAN IS **WORKING!**

OUR MILITARY OBJECTIVE . . . TO
CAUSE WIDESPREAD FEAR AND
PANIC HAS BEEN ACCOMPLISHED . . .
WE HAVE SWEPT ACROSS THE VALLEY
AND BACK . . . DESTROYING EVERY
FARM IN OUR PATH . . .

THE FLAT-LANDERS ARE
BECOMING DISCONNECTED . . .
THE STAR BEARER HAS **HELPED**
BY SOWING SEEDS OF DISTRUST
AGAINST THE DRAGONS!

REACH OUT!
DO YOU NOT **FEEL** IT?
THE BALANCE IS **SHIFTING!**
SOON YOU WILL BE **FREE** . . .

*YES . . . IT IS
TRUE . . .
WE ARE COMING
CLOSER TO THE
SURFACE . . .*

THEN HEAR ME, O LORD . . .
THE PRINCESS SURELY HAS THE
POWER TO **FREE** YOU . . .
BUT SHE ALSO HAS THE
STRENGTH TO **DESTROY YOU** - -

*. . . PERHAPS
YOU ARE
JEALOUS OF THE
PRINCESS AND THAT
IS WHY YOU
PREFER THE STAR
BEARER . . .*

MASTER . . . I AM BUT
YOUR HUMBLE SERVANT . . .
I MERELY PROPOSE THAT THE
VENI-YAN-CARI IS MORE
POWERFUL AND POSES
A GREATER **RISK**
SHOULD IT BECOME
NECESSARY TO PERFORM
A **SACRIFICE** . . .

*AND SHE
WOULD
TAKE YOUR
PLACE AS OUR
EYES AND
HANDS . . .*

PLEASE . . . MY LORD,
IF YOU COULD SEE THE **OMEN** . . .
YOU WOULD KNOW THAT THE
ONE WHO BEARS THE STAR
IS A VENI-YAN-CARI . . .
THE TWO OF US **WILL** BE
ABLE TO SHIFT THE DREAMING
. . . AND WITH LESS
RISK TO YOURSELF.

*YES . . .
YOU ARE RIGHT . . .*

YES . . .

*FOR NOW
AT LEAST . . .
YOU ARE OUR
EYES . . .*

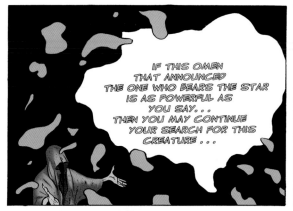

WOULD YOU GUYS MIND KEEPIN' IT **DOWN** IN HERE?

OOPS! SORRY, TED.

AIN'T IT HARD ENOUGH I'M **PATROLLIN'** THE AREA TRYIN' TO KEEP YOU GUYS **UN-SEEN**, YOU GOTTA GO ALL WHOOPIN' IT UP SO I GOTTA KEEP YA **UN-HEARD TOO**?!

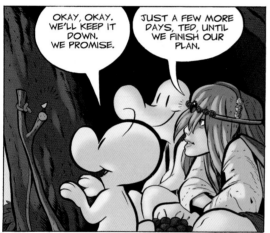

OKAY, OKAY. WE'LL KEEP IT DOWN. WE PROMISE.

JUST A FEW MORE DAYS, TED, UNTIL WE FINISH OUR PLAN.

PLAN? THE ONLY THING I SEE YOU PLANNIN' IS A RAID ON TH' SURROUNDIN' **CHERRY TREES!**

THESE WARM SUMMER DAYS AIN'T GONNA LAST FOREVER, THORN. YOU DON'T **HURRY UP**, WE GONNA BE HIDIN' FROM THE RAT CREATURES IN A **SNOWBANK!**

WE'RE NOT **HIDING**. OUR PLAN IS TO **ATTACK** THE HOODED ONE.

ATTACK HIM, HUH? JES' TH' **FOUR** OF US? WE GONNA WALK RIGHT INTO TH' RAT CREATURES' CAMP AN' JES' **POP** TH' HOODED ONE ON TH' **CHOPS**?

NO, TED, OF COURSE NOT. YOU KNOW BETTER THAN THAT.

I'M NOT SURE I **DO!** IF ANYBODY WANTS **MY** ADVICE, AN' CLEARLY NO ONE **DOES,** I SAY WE NEED TO GET TO **OLD MAN'S CAVE!**

HE'S **RIGHT,** THORN. WE CAN'T DO THIS ALONE. GRAN'MA BEN AND ALL THE VILLAGERS ARE **THERE.**

I TOLD YOU, FONE BONE, WE'RE NOT GOING TO OLD MAN'S CAVE. THERE'S NO ONE THERE WE CAN **TRUST.**

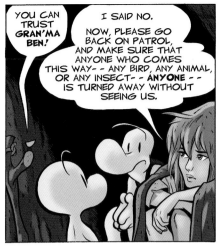

YOU CAN TRUST **GRAN'MA BEN!**

I SAID NO.

NOW, PLEASE GO BACK ON PATROL, AND MAKE SURE THAT ANYONE WHO COMES THIS WAY- - ANY BIRD, ANY ANIMAL, OR ANY INSECT- - **ANYONE** - - IS TURNED AWAY WITHOUT SEEING US.

ALL RIGHT, I'M **GOIN'.** BUT WHEN THIS IS ALL OVER, GRAN'MA BEN GONNA SQUISH ME LIKE A **BUG** FOR DISOBEYIN' HER.

ARE YOU **SURE** ABOUT GRAN'MA BEN? 'CAUSE TO TELL TH' **TRUTH,** I KINDA **MISS** HER.

EXCUSE ME. . . I'M GOING TO FIX SOME SUPPER. WOULD YOU MIND HANDING ME SOME OF THAT FUEL, SMILEY?

YEAH, OKAY. . .

IT'S JUST THAT MAYBE I DON'T UNDERSTAND TH' **PLAN.**

COULD YOU MAKE A LITTLE PILE WITH THOSE DROPPINGS?

DROPPINGS?

EEYUU!

DRIED ANIMAL DROPPINGS.

MAKES A SMOKELESS FIRE.

WE CAN WORK ON OUR PLAN WHILE WE EAT.

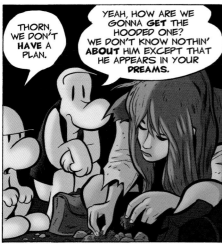

THORN, WE DON'T **HAVE** A PLAN.

YEAH, HOW ARE WE GONNA **GET** THE HOODED ONE? WE DON'T KNOW NOTHIN' **ABOUT** HIM EXCEPT THAT HE APPEARS IN YOUR **DREAMS.**

WE KNOW HE HAS AN **ARMY** THAT'S OUT HUNTING FOR YOU AND OUR COUSIN PHONEY BONE.

YEAH, THORN, WHO **IS** THIS GUY, ANYWAY?

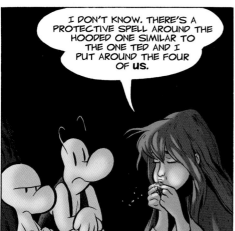

I DON'T KNOW. THERE'S A PROTECTIVE SPELL AROUND THE HOODED ONE SIMILAR TO THE ONE TED AND I PUT AROUND THE FOUR OF **US.**

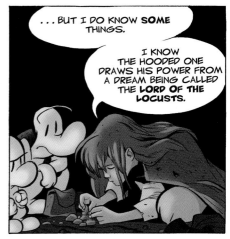

. . . BUT I DO KNOW **SOME** THINGS.

I KNOW THE HOODED ONE DRAWS HIS POWER FROM A DREAM BEING CALLED THE **LORD OF THE LOCUSTS.**

THESE POWERS LET THE HOODED ONE TRAVEL IN - -AND IN SOME CASES EVEN **PERVERT** - - OTHER PEOPLE'S DREAMS.

THE MORE FEAR HE CAUSES, THE MORE POWERFUL HE BECOMES!

SO WHY'S HE WANT YOU AN' PHONEY?

I **BELIEVE** HE WANTS US BOTH FOR THE SAME PURPOSE . . . TO SPEED THE RELEASE OF HIS **MASTER**, THE LORD OF THE LOCUSTS, WHO IS TRAPPED IN **STONE**.

THE HOODED ONE THINKS YOUR COUSIN AND I HAVE THE POWER TO HELP FREE HIM.

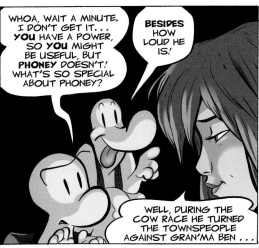

WHOA, WAIT A MINUTE. I DON'T GET IT . . . **YOU** HAVE A POWER, SO **YOU** MIGHT BE USEFUL, BUT **PHONEY** DOESN'T! WHAT'S SO SPECIAL ABOUT PHONEY?

BESIDES HOW LOUD HE IS!

WELL, DURING THE COW RACE HE TURNED THE TOWNSPEOPLE AGAINST GRAN'MA BEN . . .

THEN HE RILED UP FEAR AND ANGER AT THE **DRAGONS** FOR HIS DRAGONSLAYER SCAM!

THAT'S **EXACTLY** THE KIND OF THING THAT FEEDS THE HOODED ONE'S POWERS.

WE KNOW HE CAUSES TROUBLE, BUT - -

BOY, DO WE KNOW!

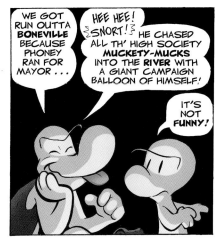

WE GOT RUN OUTTA **BONEVILLE** BECAUSE PHONEY RAN FOR MAYOR . . .

HEE HEE! *SNORT!* HE CHASED ALL TH' HIGH SOCIETY **MUCKETY-MUCKS** INTO THE **RIVER** WITH A GIANT CAMPAIGN BALLOON OF HIMSELF!

IT'S NOT **FUNNY!**

IT WAS SORTA FUNNY WHEN THE ANGRY MOB ATE A BUNCH OF PHONEY'S ROTTEN **PRUNE TARTS**, AN' HAD TO LEAVE IN A HURRY!

MY **POINT** IS THAT PHONEY WOULD NEVER DO ANYTHING TO HELP THE HOODED ONE **ON PURPOSE!**

I BELIEVE THAT. I DO . . .

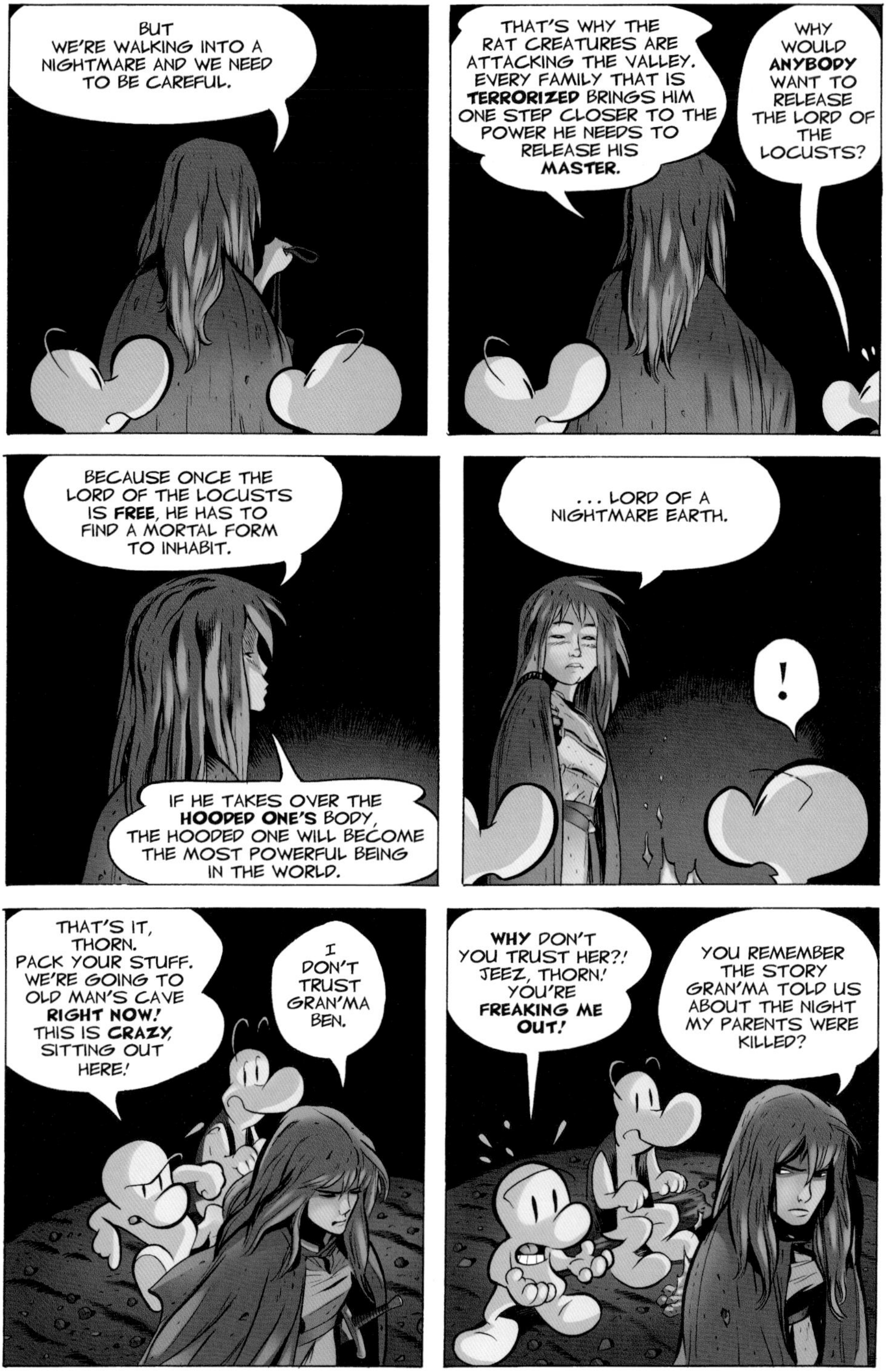
BUT WE'RE WALKING INTO A NIGHTMARE AND WE NEED TO BE CAREFUL.
THAT'S WHY THE RAT CREATURES ARE ATTACKING THE VALLEY. EVERY FAMILY THAT IS **TERRORIZED** BRINGS HIM ONE STEP CLOSER TO THE POWER HE NEEDS TO RELEASE HIS **MASTER.**
WHY WOULD **ANYBODY** WANT TO RELEASE THE LORD OF THE LOCUSTS?
BECAUSE ONCE THE LORD OF THE LOCUSTS IS **FREE**, HE HAS TO FIND A MORTAL FORM TO INHABIT.
IF HE TAKES OVER THE **HOODED ONE'S** BODY, THE HOODED ONE WILL BECOME THE MOST POWERFUL BEING IN THE WORLD.
. . . LORD OF A NIGHTMARE EARTH.
!
THAT'S IT, THORN. PACK YOUR STUFF. WE'RE GOING TO OLD MAN'S CAVE **RIGHT NOW!** THIS IS **CRAZY**, SITTING OUT HERE!
I DON'T TRUST GRAN'MA BEN.
WHY DON'T YOU TRUST HER?! JEEZ, THORN! YOU'RE **FREAKING ME OUT!**
YOU REMEMBER THE STORY GRAN'MA TOLD US ABOUT THE NIGHT MY PARENTS WERE KILLED?

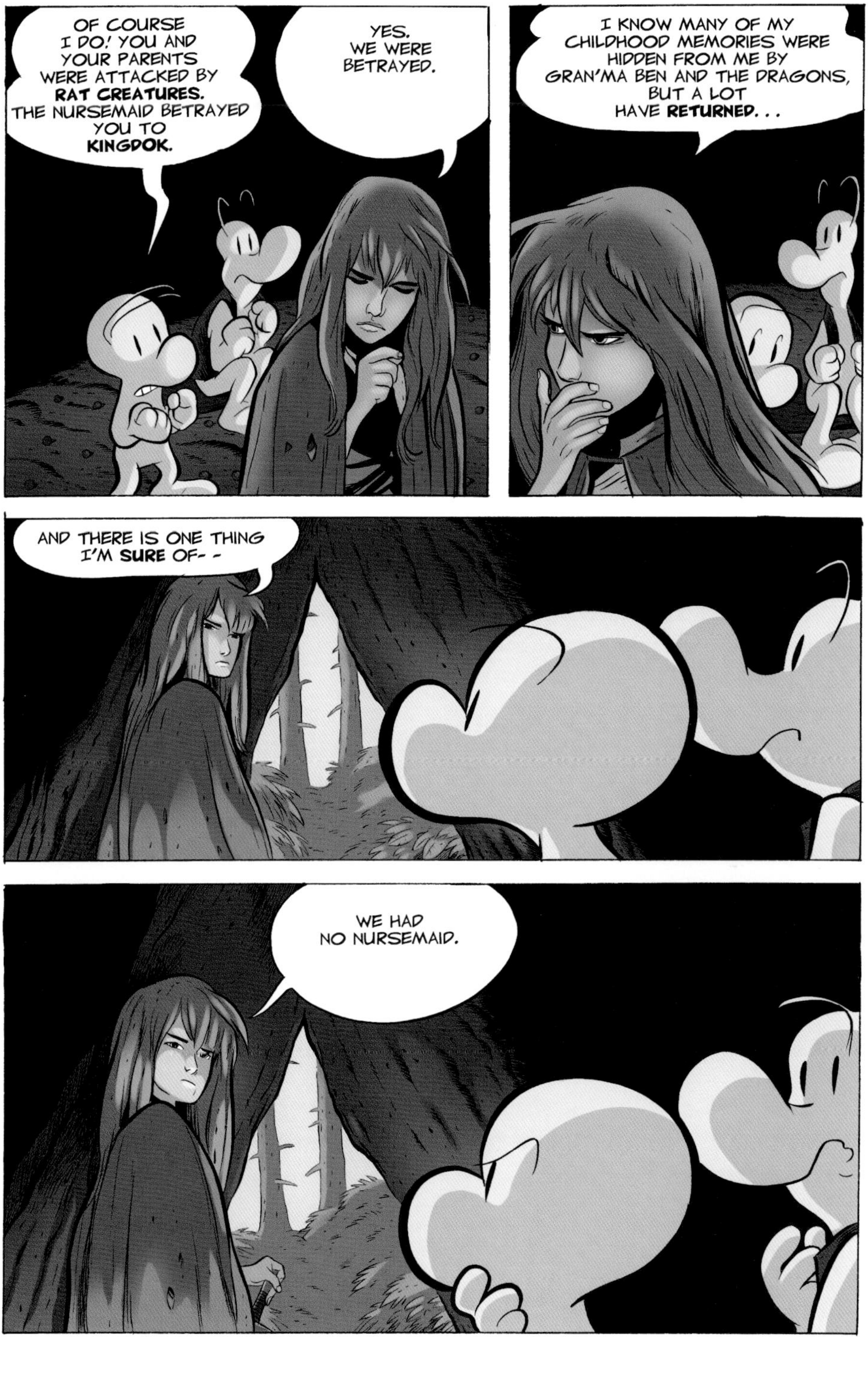
OF COURSE I DO! YOU AND YOUR PARENTS WERE ATTACKED BY **RAT CREATURES.** THE NURSEMAID BETRAYED YOU TO **KINGDOK.**
YES. WE WERE BETRAYED.
I KNOW MANY OF MY CHILDHOOD MEMORIES WERE HIDDEN FROM ME BY GRAN'MA BEN AND THE DRAGONS, BUT A LOT HAVE **RETURNED**. . .
AND THERE IS ONE THING I'M **SURE** OF- -
WE HAD NO NURSEMAID.

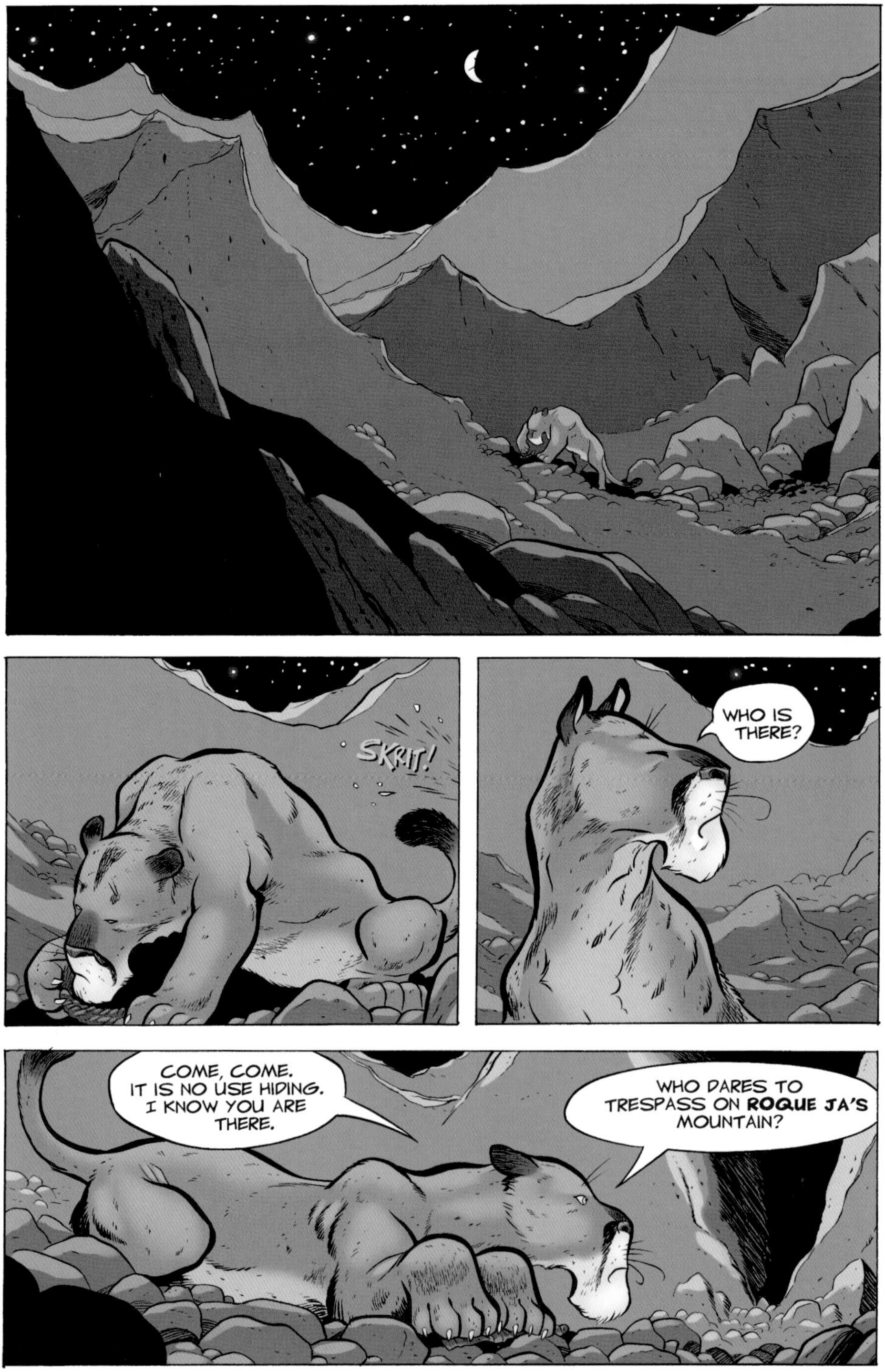
SKRIT!
WHO IS THERE?
COME, COME. IT IS NO USE HIDING. I KNOW YOU ARE THERE.
WHO DARES TO TRESPASS ON **ROQUE JA'S** MOUNTAIN?

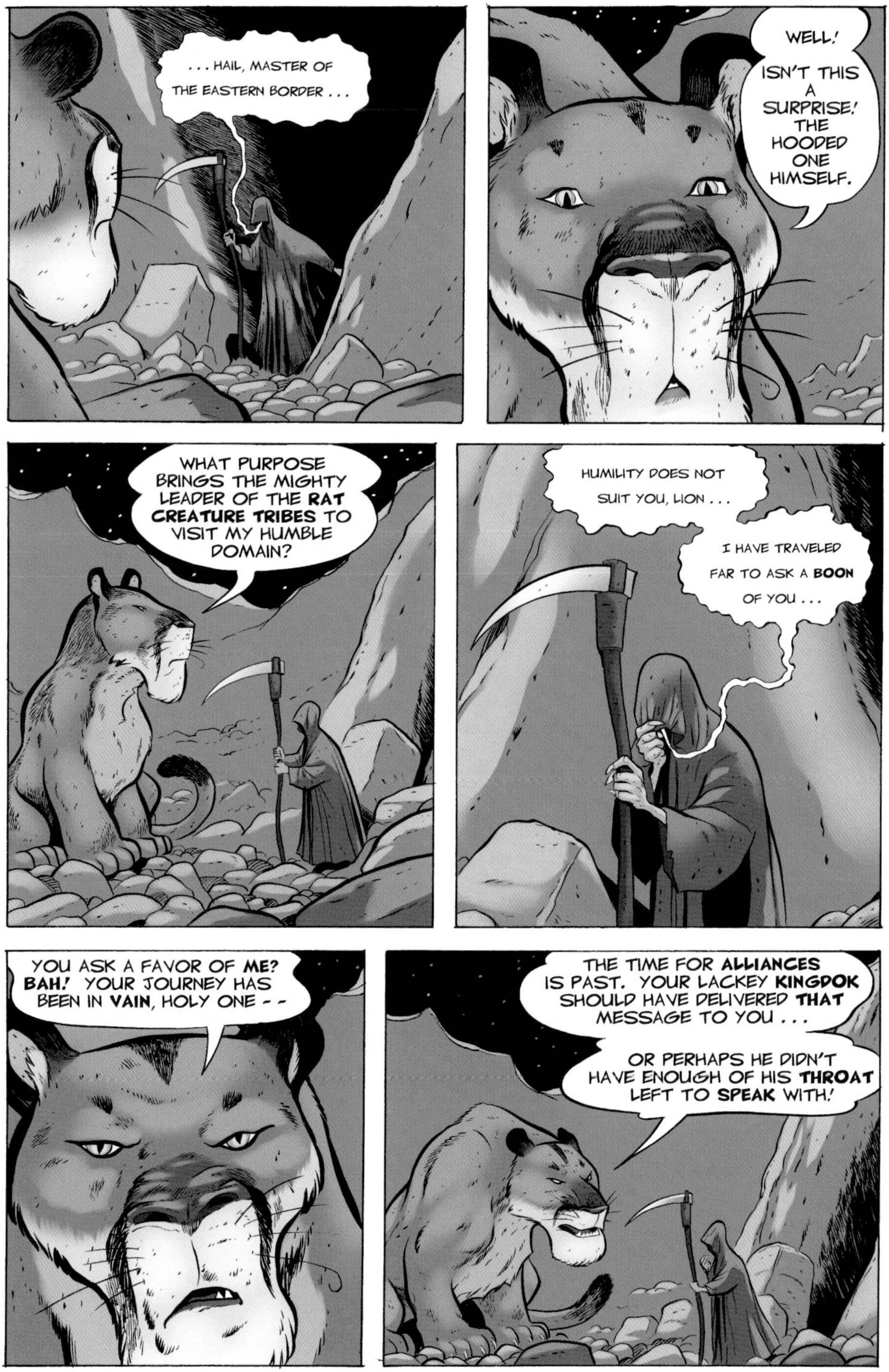
. . . HAIL, MASTER OF THE EASTERN BORDER . . .
WELL! ISN'T THIS A SURPRISE! THE HOODED ONE HIMSELF.
WHAT PURPOSE BRINGS THE MIGHTY LEADER OF THE **RAT CREATURE TRIBES** TO VISIT MY HUMBLE DOMAIN?
HUMILITY DOES NOT SUIT YOU, LION . . .
I HAVE TRAVELED FAR TO ASK A **BOON** OF YOU . . .
YOU ASK A FAVOR OF **ME? BAH!** YOUR JOURNEY HAS BEEN IN **VAIN**, HOLY ONE - -
THE TIME FOR **ALLIANCES** IS PAST. YOUR LACKEY **KINGDOK** SHOULD HAVE DELIVERED **THAT** MESSAGE TO YOU . . .
OR PERHAPS HE DIDN'T HAVE ENOUGH OF HIS **THROAT** LEFT TO **SPEAK** WITH!

YES, I'VE CAPTURED THEM. . . **TWICE**, IN FACT. WHAT DO YOU WANT THEM FOR?

THAT IS MY CONCERN. . . BUT TIME IS RUNNING SHORT. . . . . . I MUST HAVE THEM BEFORE THE HARVEST MOON . . .

CAN YOU **DELIVER** THEM?

THE HARVEST MOON? **BLOOD MOON**, YOU MEAN. WHAT ARE YOU UP TO, STICK-EATER?

ARE YOU PLANNING A RITUAL? A **SACRIFICE**, PERHAPS?

ALL MAGIC IS STRONGER WHEN ONE USES THE NATURAL WAXING AND WANING OF THE DREAMING RHYTHMS . . .

ANSWER ME, ROGUE JA . . . WILL YOU DO THIS THING FOR ME?

I TRIED TO GIVE THEM TO YOU ONCE **ALREADY**. BUT **KINGDOK** INSISTED I LEAVE THEM WITHOUT PROPER **COMPENSATION**.

I DID END UP WITH HIS **TONGUE**, OF COURSE, BUT I WILL WANT **MORE** NEXT TIME.

YOU WILL BE REWARDED. . . NAME YOUR PRICE.

I WILL HAVE COMPLETE SOVEREIGNTY OVER THE EASTERN MOUNTAINS **NORTH** OF THE OLD TEMPLE.

DONE.

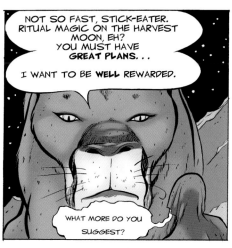

NOT SO FAST, STICK-EATER. RITUAL MAGIC ON THE HARVEST MOON, EH? YOU MUST HAVE **GREAT PLANS**. . .

I WANT TO BE **WELL** REWARDED.

WHAT MORE DO YOU SUGGEST?

A **TRIBUTE**. ONCE A YEAR YOUR HAIRY MEN WILL BRING TO ME ONE **EIGHTH** OF THEIR SPOILS.

YOU WILL HAVE A **FULL QUARTER** IF YOU ALSO BRING TO ME THE **DEAD BODY OF THE PRINCESS**.

WHA- - ?

THE DEAD BODY OF THE PRINCESS? OF WHAT USE IS A **DEAD BODY** AT A **SACRIFICE**?

LET US JUST SAY THAT I DO NOT WISH THERE TO BE ANY **RIVALS** AT MY PARTY. DO WE HAVE A DEAL?

DONE. I WILL BRING YOU YOUR BONE CREATURES.

AND YOUR DEAD PRINCESS.

I WILL BE WAITING.

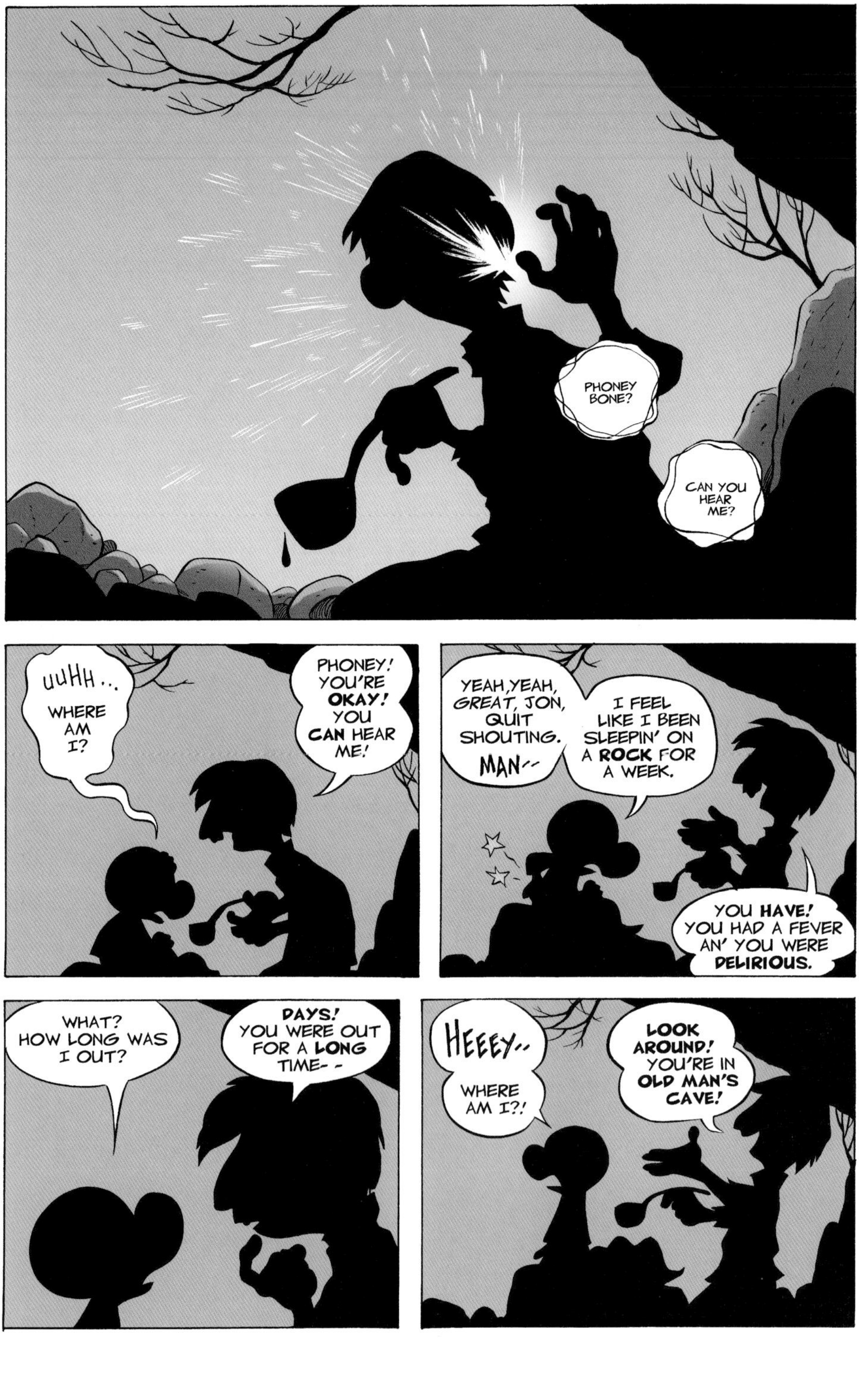
PHONEY BONE?
CAN YOU HEAR ME?
UUHH... WHERE AM I?
PHONEY! YOU'RE OKAY! YOU CAN HEAR ME!
YEAH, YEAH, GREAT, JON, QUIT SHOUTING. MAN--
I FEEL LIKE I BEEN SLEEPIN' ON A ROCK FOR A WEEK.
YOU HAVE! YOU HAD A FEVER AN' YOU WERE DELIRIOUS.
WHAT? HOW LONG WAS I OUT?
DAYS! YOU WERE OUT FOR A LONG TIME- -
HEEEY.. WHERE AM I?!
LOOK AROUND! YOU'RE IN OLD MAN'S CAVE!

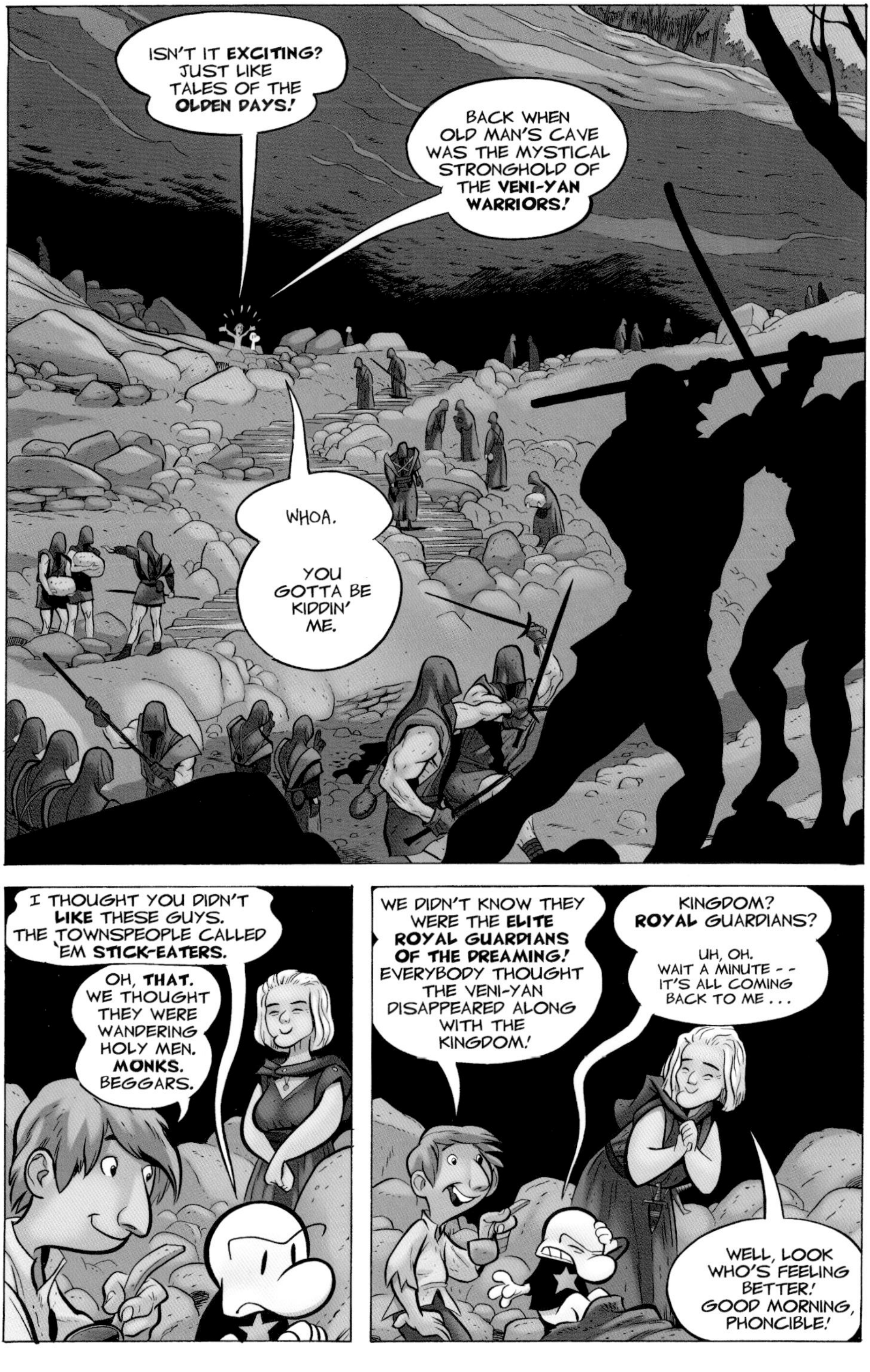
ISN'T IT EXCITING? JUST LIKE TALES OF THE OLDEN DAYS!
BACK WHEN OLD MAN'S CAVE WAS THE MYSTICAL STRONGHOLD OF THE VENI-YAN WARRIORS!
WHOA.
YOU GOTTA BE KIDDIN' ME.
I THOUGHT YOU DIDN'T LIKE THESE GUYS. THE TOWNSPEOPLE CALLED 'EM STICK-EATERS.
OH, THAT. WE THOUGHT THEY WERE WANDERING HOLY MEN. MONKS. BEGGARS.
WE DIDN'T KNOW THEY WERE THE ELITE ROYAL GUARDIANS OF THE DREAMING! EVERYBODY THOUGHT THE VENI-YAN DISAPPEARED ALONG WITH THE KINGDOM!
KINGDOM? ROYAL GUARDIANS?
UH, OH. WAIT A MINUTE - - IT'S ALL COMING BACK TO ME . . .
WELL, LOOK WHO'S FEELING BETTER! GOOD MORNING, PHONCIBLE!

WHEN WE **DREAM**, WE PEER THROUGH A FOGGY GLASS INTO THE RIVER AND SEE A WORLD THAT IS CONNECTED TO ALL OTHER LIVING THINGS.

THAT DREAMING WORLD EXISTS EVEN WHEN WE ARE AWAKE.

YOU'RE STARTIN' TO SCARE ME, GRAN'MA.

THERE'S MORE TO THE WORLD THAN WHAT YOU SEE WITH YOUR EYES, PHONCIBLE.

PFFF!

NOTHIN' **IMPORTANT.**

YOU ARE, WITHOUT A **DOUBT,** THE MOST MATERIALISTIC PERSON I KNOW.

COME. I WANT TO SHOW YOU SOMETHING.

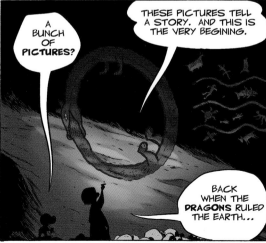

A BUNCH OF PICTURES?

THESE PICTURES TELL A STORY. AND THIS IS THE VERY BEGINING.

BACK WHEN THE **DRAGONS** RULED THE EARTH...

WHEN THE WORLD WAS VERY, VERY NEW, THE **FIRST** DRAGON WAS A QUEEN NAMED **MIM**. MIM MAINTAINED THE DREAMING BY WATCHING ITS FLOW AND KEEPING IT **BALANCED**.

THE **DREAMING** IS A THING OF GREAT DELICACY, AND BALANCE IS MOST IMPORTANT.

MIM WATCHED THE DREAMING WITH **CARE**, AND ALL CREATURES LIVED TOGETHER IN PEACE AND HARMONY. . .

. . . UNTIL ONE DAY A SPIRIT KNOWN AS THE **LORD OF THE LOCUSTS** BECAME UNHAPPY.

THE LORD OF THE LOCUSTS WAS A NIGHTMARE BEING WITHOUT **SHAPE** OR **FORM** WHO COULD EXIST ONLY IN THE SPIRIT WORLD.

BUT HE WANTED TO MOVE IN **OUR** WORLD TOO, AND TO DO **THAT** - - TO BECOME PART OF OUR **CRUDE** REALITY - - HE WOULD HAVE TO TAKE POSSESSION OF A **MORTAL BEING'S FLESH!**

HE CHOSE **MIM**, **QUEEN OF THE DRAGONS**, THE MOST POWERFUL DREAMER IN THE WORLD.

DRAGONS AREN'T **IMMORTAL?**

DRAGONS LIVE FOR A VERY LONG TIME, BUT THEY ARE MORTAL. EVERYTHING IN **OUR** WORLD IS MORTAL.

THE LORD OF THE LOCUSTS ENTERED HER MIND AND THE QUEEN OF THE DRAGONS WENT **MAD**. BALANCE WAS **LOST**, AND THE WORLD WENT DARK.

TO SAVE THE WORLD, ALL THE OTHER DRAGONS HAD TO MOVE **AGAINST** HER! THEY TURNED HER TO **STONE**, AND THEY **TRAPPED** THE LORD OF THE LOCUSTS INSIDE HER **FOREVER!**

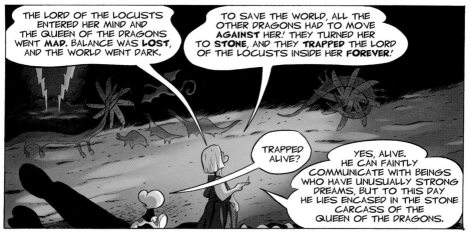

TRAPPED ALIVE?

YES, ALIVE. HE CAN FAINTLY COMMUNICATE WITH BEINGS WHO HAVE UNUSUALLY STRONG DREAMS, BUT TO THIS DAY HE LIES ENCASED IN THE STONE CARCASS OF THE QUEEN OF THE DRAGONS.

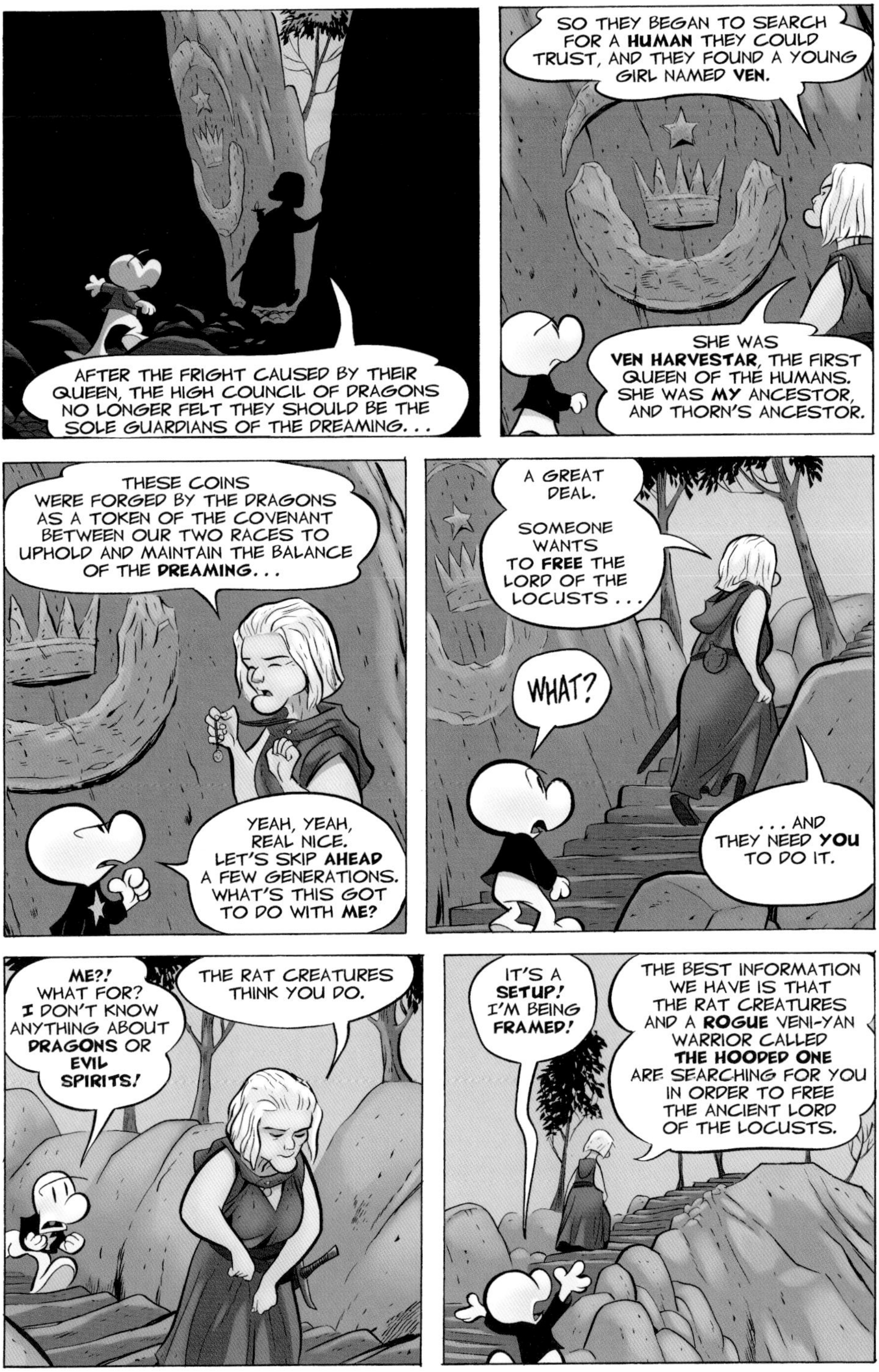
AFTER THE FRIGHT CAUSED BY THEIR QUEEN, THE HIGH COUNCIL OF DRAGONS NO LONGER FELT THEY SHOULD BE THE SOLE GUARDIANS OF THE DREAMING. . .
SO THEY BEGAN TO SEARCH FOR A HUMAN THEY COULD TRUST, AND THEY FOUND A YOUNG GIRL NAMED VEN.
SHE WAS VEN HARVESTAR, THE FIRST QUEEN OF THE HUMANS. SHE WAS MY ANCESTOR, AND THORN'S ANCESTOR.
THESE COINS WERE FORGED BY THE DRAGONS AS A TOKEN OF THE COVENANT BETWEEN OUR TWO RACES TO UPHOLD AND MAINTAIN THE BALANCE OF THE DREAMING. . .
YEAH, YEAH, REAL NICE. LET'S SKIP AHEAD A FEW GENERATIONS. WHAT'S THIS GOT TO DO WITH ME?
A GREAT DEAL.
SOMEONE WANTS TO FREE THE LORD OF THE LOCUSTS . . .
WHAT?
. . . AND THEY NEED YOU TO DO IT.
ME?! WHAT FOR? I DON'T KNOW ANYTHING ABOUT DRAGONS OR EVIL SPIRITS!
THE RAT CREATURES THINK YOU DO.
IT'S A SETUP! I'M BEING FRAMED!
THE BEST INFORMATION WE HAVE IS THAT THE RAT CREATURES AND A ROGUE VENI-YAN WARRIOR CALLED THE HOODED ONE ARE SEARCHING FOR YOU IN ORDER TO FREE THE ANCIENT LORD OF THE LOCUSTS.

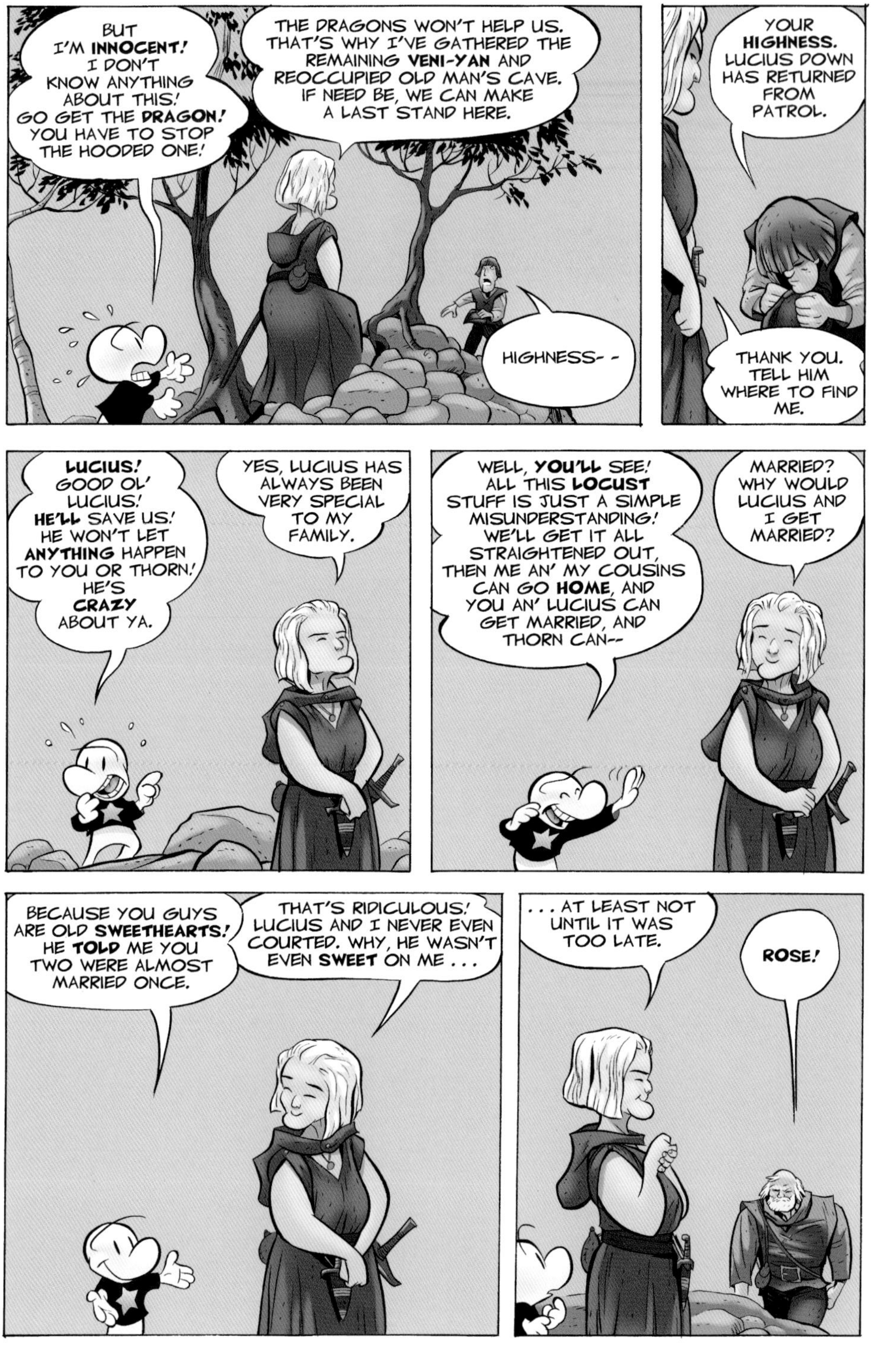
BUT I'M INNOCENT! I DON'T KNOW ANYTHING ABOUT THIS! GO GET THE DRAGON! YOU HAVE TO STOP THE HOODED ONE!
THE DRAGONS WON'T HELP US. THAT'S WHY I'VE GATHERED THE REMAINING VENI-YAN AND REOCCUPIED OLD MAN'S CAVE. IF NEED BE, WE CAN MAKE A LAST STAND HERE.
HIGHNESS- -
YOUR HIGHNESS. LUCIUS DOWN HAS RETURNED FROM PATROL.
THANK YOU. TELL HIM WHERE TO FIND ME.
LUCIUS! GOOD OL' LUCIUS! HE'LL SAVE US! HE WON'T LET ANYTHING HAPPEN TO YOU OR THORN! HE'S CRAZY ABOUT YA.
YES, LUCIUS HAS ALWAYS BEEN VERY SPECIAL TO MY FAMILY.
WELL, YOU'LL SEE! ALL THIS LOCUST STUFF IS JUST A SIMPLE MISUNDERSTANDING! WE'LL GET IT ALL STRAIGHTENED OUT, THEN ME AN' MY COUSINS CAN GO HOME, AND YOU AN' LUCIUS CAN GET MARRIED, AND THORN CAN--
MARRIED? WHY WOULD LUCIUS AND I GET MARRIED?
BECAUSE YOU GUYS ARE OLD SWEETHEARTS! HE TOLD ME YOU TWO WERE ALMOST MARRIED ONCE.
THAT'S RIDICULOUS! LUCIUS AND I NEVER EVEN COURTED. WHY, HE WASN'T EVEN SWEET ON ME . . .
. . . AT LEAST NOT UNTIL IT WAS TOO LATE.
ROSE!

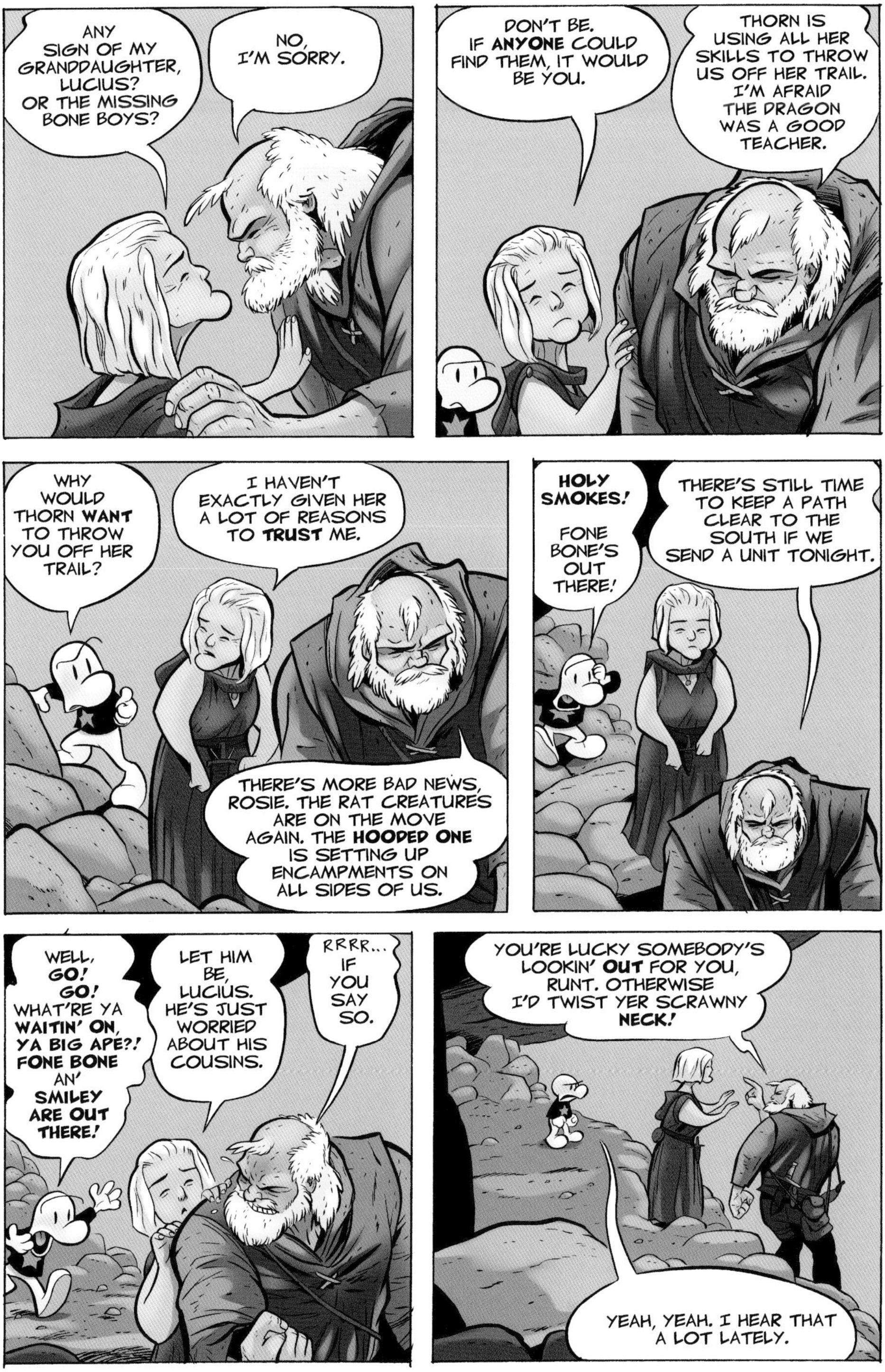
ANY SIGN OF MY GRANDDAUGHTER, LUCIUS? OR THE MISSING BONE BOYS?
NO, I'M SORRY.
DON'T BE. IF **ANYONE** COULD FIND THEM, IT WOULD BE YOU.
THORN IS USING ALL HER SKILLS TO THROW US OFF HER TRAIL. I'M AFRAID THE DRAGON WAS A GOOD TEACHER.
WHY WOULD THORN **WANT** TO THROW YOU OFF HER TRAIL?
I HAVEN'T EXACTLY GIVEN HER A LOT OF REASONS TO **TRUST** ME.
THERE'S MORE BAD NEWS, ROSIE. THE RAT CREATURES ARE ON THE MOVE AGAIN. THE **HOODED ONE** IS SETTING UP ENCAMPMENTS ON ALL SIDES OF US.
HOLY SMOKES! FONE BONE'S OUT THERE!
THERE'S STILL TIME TO KEEP A PATH CLEAR TO THE SOUTH IF WE SEND A UNIT TONIGHT.
WELL, **GO! GO!** WHAT'RE YA **WAITIN' ON, YA BIG APE?! FONE BONE** AN' **SMILEY ARE OUT THERE!**
LET HIM BE, LUCIUS. HE'S JUST WORRIED ABOUT HIS COUSINS.
RRRR... IF YOU SAY SO.
YOU'RE LUCKY SOMEBODY'S LOOKIN' **OUT** FOR YOU, RUNT. OTHERWISE I'D TWIST YER SCRAWNY **NECK!**
YEAH, YEAH. I HEAR THAT A LOT LATELY.

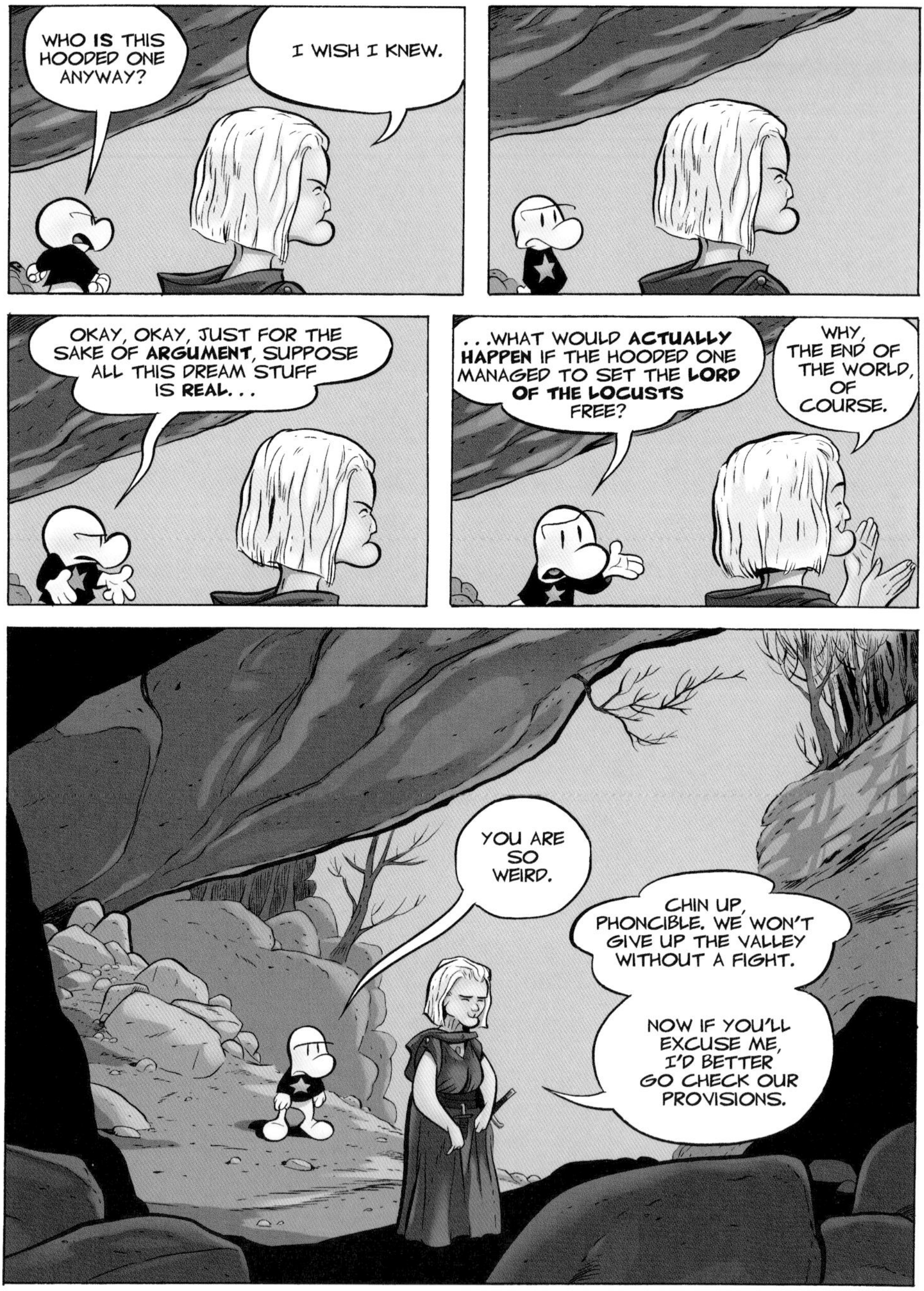
WHO IS THIS HOODED ONE ANYWAY?
I WISH I KNEW.
OKAY, OKAY, JUST FOR THE SAKE OF ARGUMENT, SUPPOSE ALL THIS DREAM STUFF IS REAL. . .
. . .WHAT WOULD ACTUALLY HAPPEN IF THE HOODED ONE MANAGED TO SET THE LORD OF THE LOCUSTS FREE?
WHY, THE END OF THE WORLD, OF COURSE.
YOU ARE SO WEIRD.
CHIN UP, PHONCIBLE. WE WON'T GIVE UP THE VALLEY WITHOUT A FIGHT.
NOW IF YOU'LL EXCUSE ME, I'D BETTER GO CHECK OUR PROVISIONS.

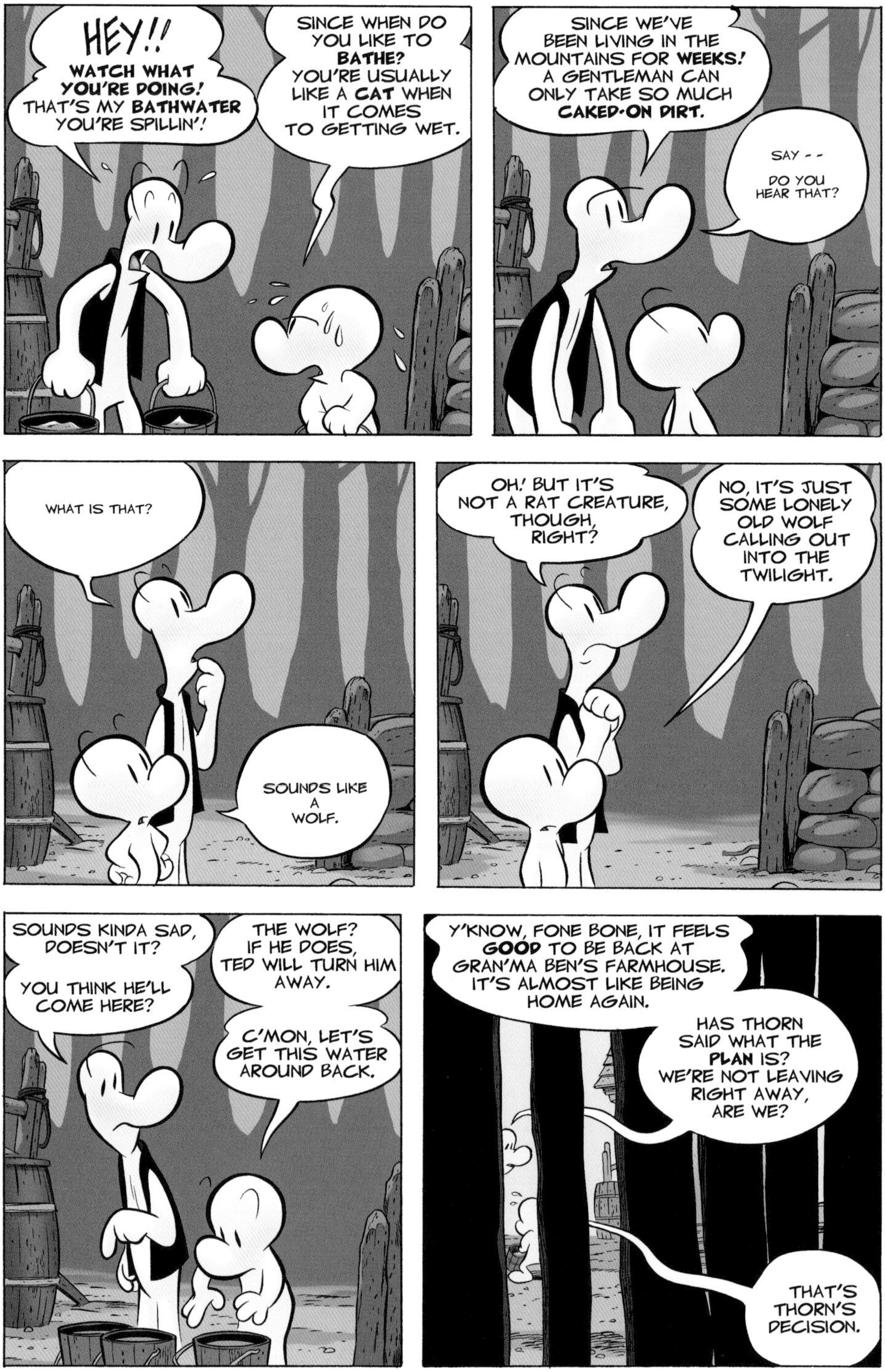
HEY!! WATCH WHAT YOU'RE DOING! THAT'S MY BATHWATER YOU'RE SPILLIN'!
SINCE WHEN DO YOU LIKE TO BATHE? YOU'RE USUALLY LIKE A CAT WHEN IT COMES TO GETTING WET.
SINCE WE'VE BEEN LIVING IN THE MOUNTAINS FOR WEEKS! A GENTLEMAN CAN ONLY TAKE SO MUCH CAKED-ON DIRT.
SAY - - DO YOU HEAR THAT?
WHAT IS THAT?
SOUNDS LIKE A WOLF.
OH! BUT IT'S NOT A RAT CREATURE, THOUGH, RIGHT?
NO, IT'S JUST SOME LONELY OLD WOLF CALLING OUT INTO THE TWILIGHT.
SOUNDS KINDA SAD, DOESN'T IT?
YOU THINK HE'LL COME HERE?
THE WOLF? IF HE DOES, TED WILL TURN HIM AWAY.
C'MON, LET'S GET THIS WATER AROUND BACK.
Y'KNOW, FONE BONE, IT FEELS GOOD TO BE BACK AT GRAN'MA BEN'S FARMHOUSE. IT'S ALMOST LIKE BEING HOME AGAIN.
HAS THORN SAID WHAT THE PLAN IS? WE'RE NOT LEAVING RIGHT AWAY, ARE WE?
THAT'S THORN'S DECISION.

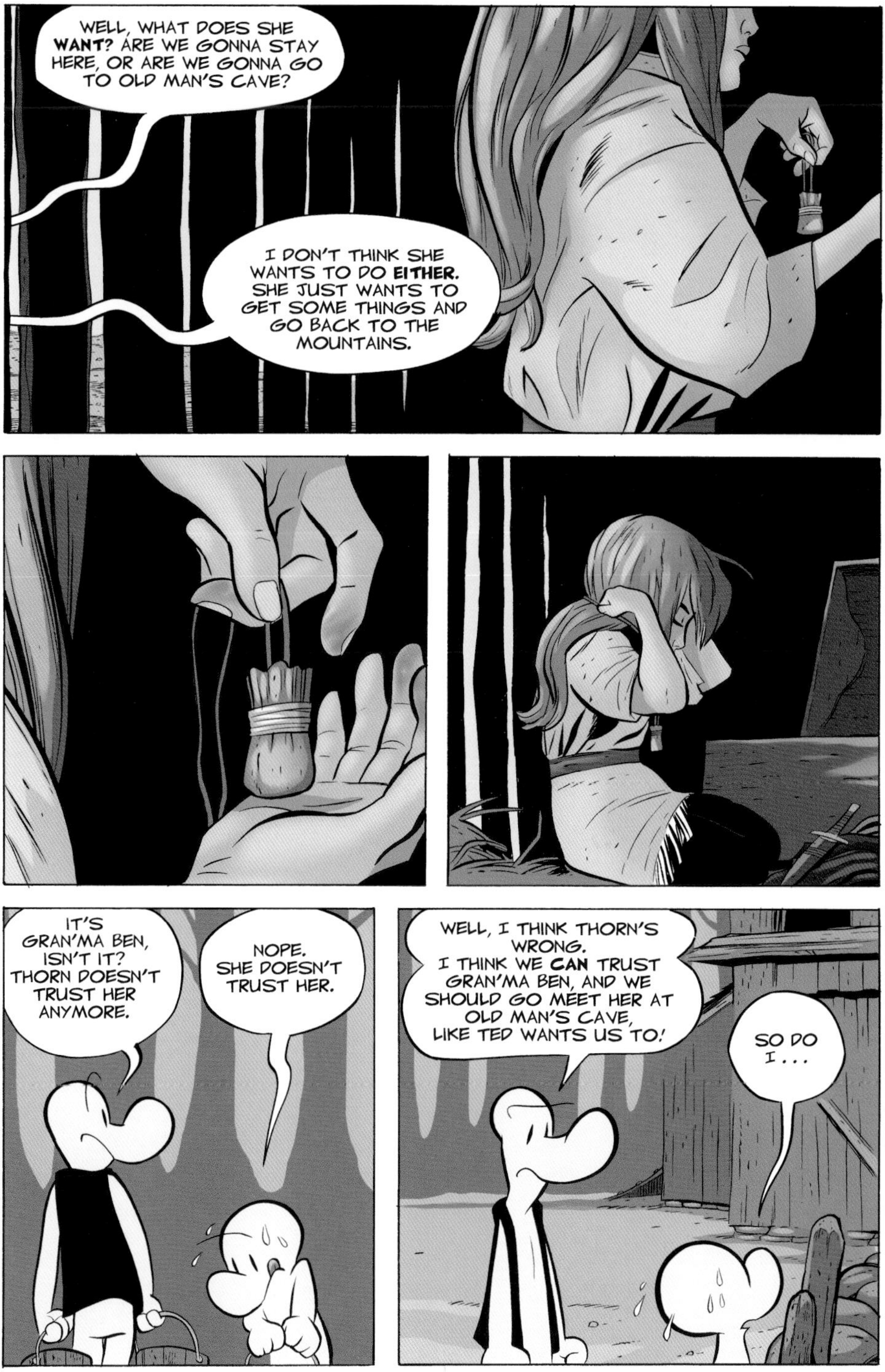
WELL, WHAT DOES SHE **WANT?** ARE WE GONNA STAY HERE, OR ARE WE GONNA GO TO OLD MAN'S CAVE?
I DON'T THINK SHE WANTS TO DO **EITHER.** SHE JUST WANTS TO GET SOME THINGS AND GO BACK TO THE MOUNTAINS.
IT'S GRAN'MA BEN, ISN'T IT? THORN DOESN'T TRUST HER ANYMORE.
NOPE. SHE DOESN'T TRUST HER.
WELL, I THINK THORN'S WRONG. I THINK WE **CAN** TRUST GRAN'MA BEN, AND WE SHOULD GO MEET HER AT OLD MAN'S CAVE, LIKE TED WANTS US TO!
SO DO I . . .

...BUT UNTIL THORN CHANGES HER MIND, WE'LL JUST HAVE TO BE PATIENT.

AT LEAST UNTIL WE HEAR THIS BIG **PLAN** OF HERS.

YOU THINK SHE REALLY **HAS** A PLAN?

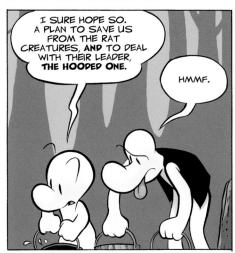

I SURE HOPE SO. A PLAN TO SAVE US FROM THE RAT CREATURES, **AND** TO DEAL WITH THEIR LEADER, **THE HOODED ONE.**

HMMF.

IF THORN **DID** HAVE A PLAN, WHY WOULDN'T SHE TELL IT TO US?

THE PLAN IS TO SNEAK INTO THE RAT CREATURES' ENCAMPMENT AND **ASSASSINATE** THE HOODED ONE...

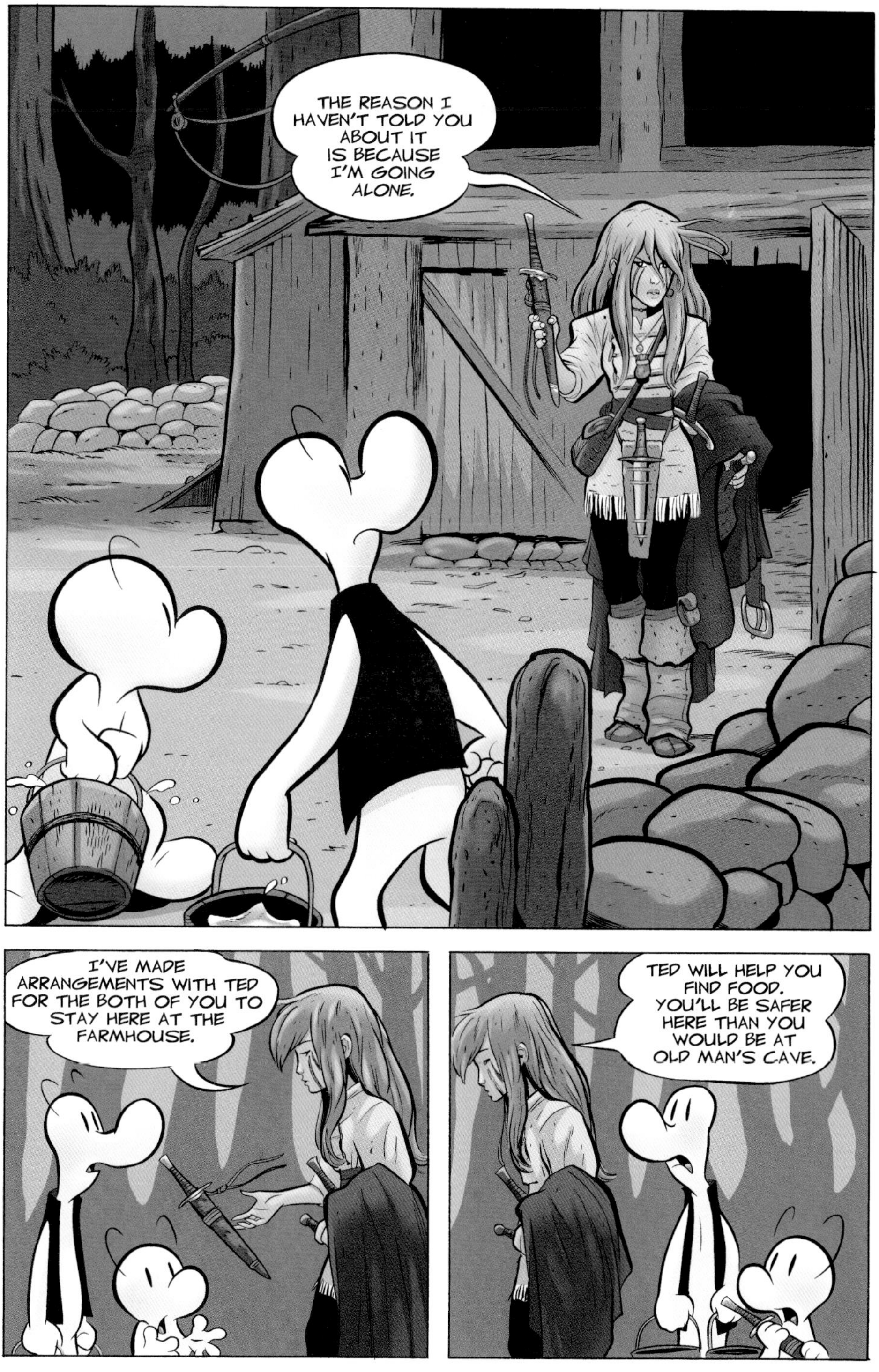
THE REASON I HAVEN'T TOLD YOU ABOUT IT IS BECAUSE I'M GOING ALONE.
I'VE MADE ARRANGEMENTS WITH TED FOR THE BOTH OF YOU TO STAY HERE AT THE FARMHOUSE.
TED WILL HELP YOU FIND FOOD. YOU'LL BE SAFER HERE THAN YOU WOULD BE AT OLD MAN'S CAVE.

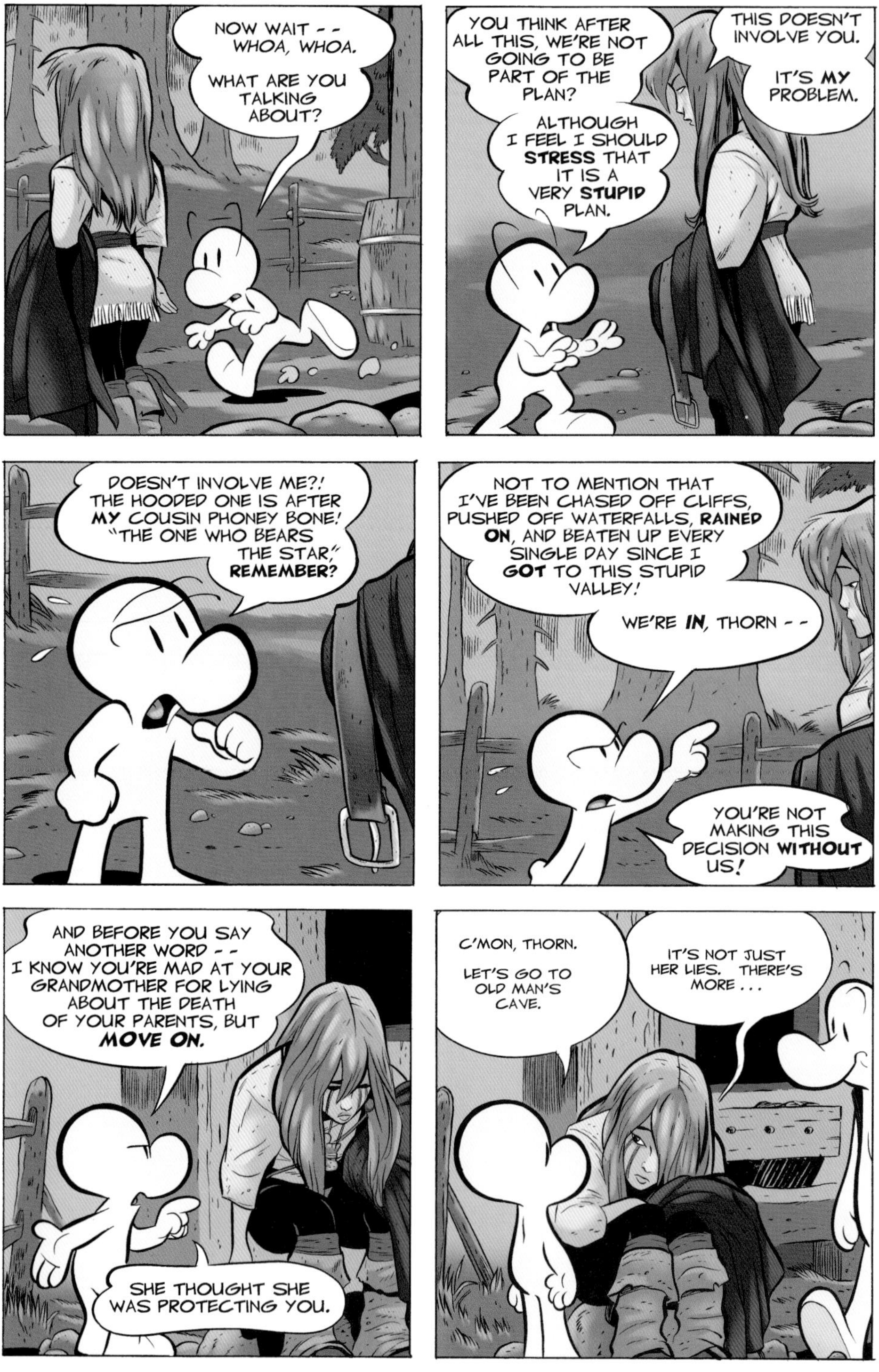
NOW WAIT - - WHOA, WHOA.
WHAT ARE YOU TALKING ABOUT?
YOU THINK AFTER ALL THIS, WE'RE NOT GOING TO BE PART OF THE PLAN?
ALTHOUGH I FEEL I SHOULD STRESS THAT IT IS A VERY STUPID PLAN.
THIS DOESN'T INVOLVE YOU.
IT'S MY PROBLEM.
DOESN'T INVOLVE ME?! THE HOODED ONE IS AFTER MY COUSIN PHONEY BONE! "THE ONE WHO BEARS THE STAR," REMEMBER?
NOT TO MENTION THAT I'VE BEEN CHASED OFF CLIFFS, PUSHED OFF WATERFALLS, RAINED ON, AND BEATEN UP EVERY SINGLE DAY SINCE I GOT TO THIS STUPID VALLEY!
WE'RE IN, THORN - -
YOU'RE NOT MAKING THIS DECISION WITHOUT US!
AND BEFORE YOU SAY ANOTHER WORD - - I KNOW YOU'RE MAD AT YOUR GRANDMOTHER FOR LYING ABOUT THE DEATH OF YOUR PARENTS, BUT MOVE ON.
SHE THOUGHT SHE WAS PROTECTING YOU.
C'MON, THORN.
LET'S GO TO OLD MAN'S CAVE.
IT'S NOT JUST HER LIES. THERE'S MORE . . .

WOLF CALL

ALMOST EVERY NIGHT GRAN'MA BEN APPEARS TO ME IN A DREAM . . .

BUT SOMETHING IS WRONG.

SHE SEEMS SPLIT IN TWO . . .

FIRST PULLING ME IN ONE DIRECTION, THEN ANOTHER. IT'S LIKE HAVING TWO DIFFERENT GRAN'MA BENS BATTLING FOR POSSESSION OF ME.

IT'S JUST A DREAM - -

IT'S **NOT** JUST A DREAM! YOU DON'T KNOW WHAT IT'S LIKE.

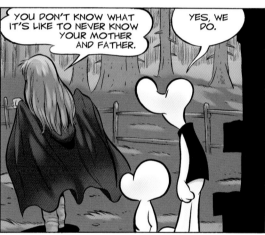

YOU DON'T KNOW WHAT IT'S LIKE TO NEVER KNOW YOUR MOTHER AND FATHER.

YES, WE DO.

WHAT DID YOU SAY?

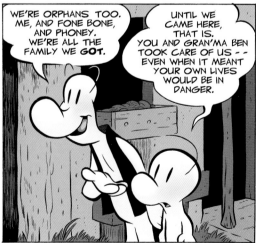

WE'RE ORPHANS TOO. ME, AND FONE BONE, AND PHONEY. WE'RE ALL THE FAMILY WE **GOT.**

UNTIL WE CAME HERE, THAT IS. YOU AND GRAN'MA BEN TOOK CARE OF US - - EVEN WHEN IT MEANT YOUR OWN LIVES WOULD BE IN DANGER.

WHEN WE WERE KIDS, PHONEY WAS THE OLDEST AND HE TOOK CARE OF US.

I ALWAYS FIGURED THAT WAS **WHY** HE GOT SO RESOURCEFUL AND STINGY.

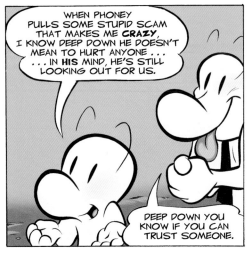

WHEN PHONEY PULLS SOME STUPID SCAM THAT MAKES ME **CRAZY**, I KNOW DEEP DOWN HE DOESN'T MEAN TO HURT ANYONE . . . . . . IN **HIS** MIND, HE'S STILL LOOKING OUT FOR US.

DEEP DOWN YOU KNOW IF YOU CAN TRUST SOMEONE.

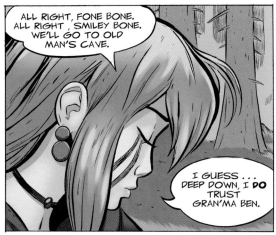

ALL RIGHT, FONE BONE. ALL RIGHT, SMILEY BONE. WE'LL GO TO OLD MAN'S CAVE.

I GUESS . . . DEEP DOWN, I **DO** TRUST GRAN'MA BEN.

GRAB YOUR STUFF, AND LET'S GO.

MAN, I HOPE YOU'RE RIGHT ABOUT THIS!

HEY, **THORN!** CAN I WEAR SOME OF THAT WAR PAINT, TOO? HUH, CAN I?

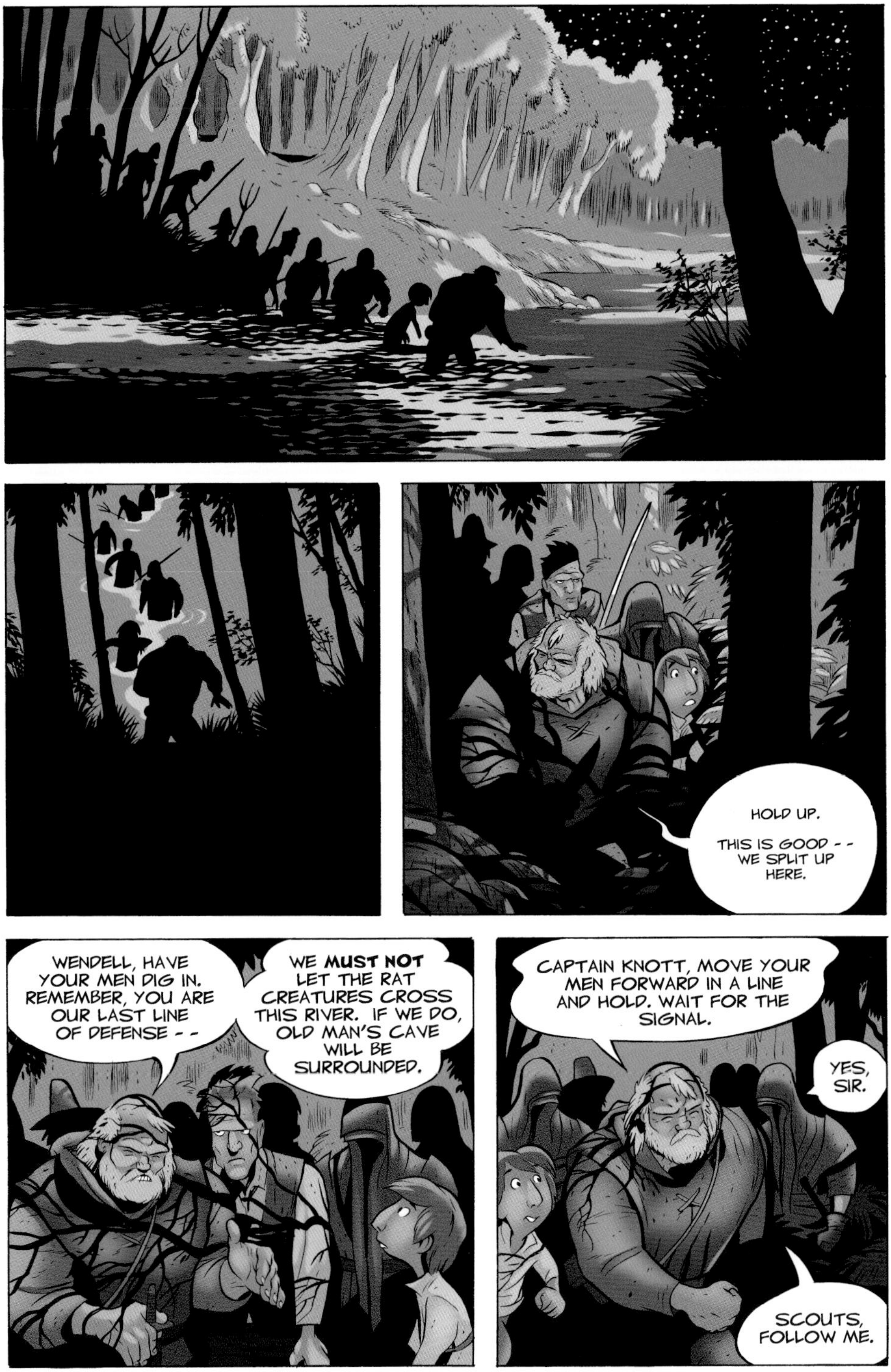
HOLD UP.
THIS IS GOOD - - WE SPLIT UP HERE.
WENDELL, HAVE YOUR MEN DIG IN. REMEMBER, YOU ARE OUR LAST LINE OF DEFENSE - -
WE **MUST NOT** LET THE RAT CREATURES CROSS THIS RIVER. IF WE DO, OLD MAN'S CAVE WILL BE SURROUNDED.
CAPTAIN KNOTT, MOVE YOUR MEN FORWARD IN A LINE AND HOLD. WAIT FOR THE SIGNAL.
YES, SIR.
SCOUTS, FOLLOW ME.

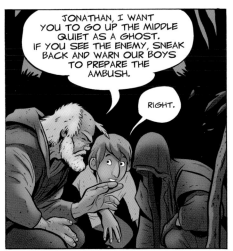

JONATHAN, I WANT YOU TO GO UP THE MIDDLE QUIET AS A GHOST. IF YOU SEE THE ENEMY, SNEAK BACK AND WARN OUR BOYS TO PREPARE THE AMBUSH.

RIGHT.

SON, YOU MOVE UP THE NORTH BANK AND KEEP YOUR EYES PEELED -- OR WHATEVER IT IS YOU DO WITH THAT HOOD PULLED OVER YOUR FACE.

WE ARE WELL TRAINED TO SEE.

VERY GOOD.

NOW, REMEMBER, DO **NOT** ENGAGE THE ENEMY! YOUR JOB IS TO WARN OUR BOYS . . .

. . . WE HAVE TO KEEP THOSE RATS FROM CROSSING THE RIVER.

LUCIUS . . .

WHO'S THERE?

DO NOT DRAW YOUR WEAPON . . . . . IT IS ME . . .

WHAT
TH - - ?

DO YOU NOT
RECOGNIZE ME?
HAS IT BEEN SO
LONG?

B - -
BRIAR?

IS IT REALLY
YOU - - ?

YES,
LUCIUS . . .
IT IS REALLY ME.
COME
CLOSER. . .

YOU CANNOT
KNOW HOW PAINFUL
IT HAS BEEN TO
BE APART FROM
YOU . . .
I HAVE
ACHED TO BE
WITH YOU . . .

TELL ME . . . HOW IS
MY BABY SISTER . . . ? HOW IS
ROSE? HAVE YOU TAKEN GOOD
CARE OF HER?

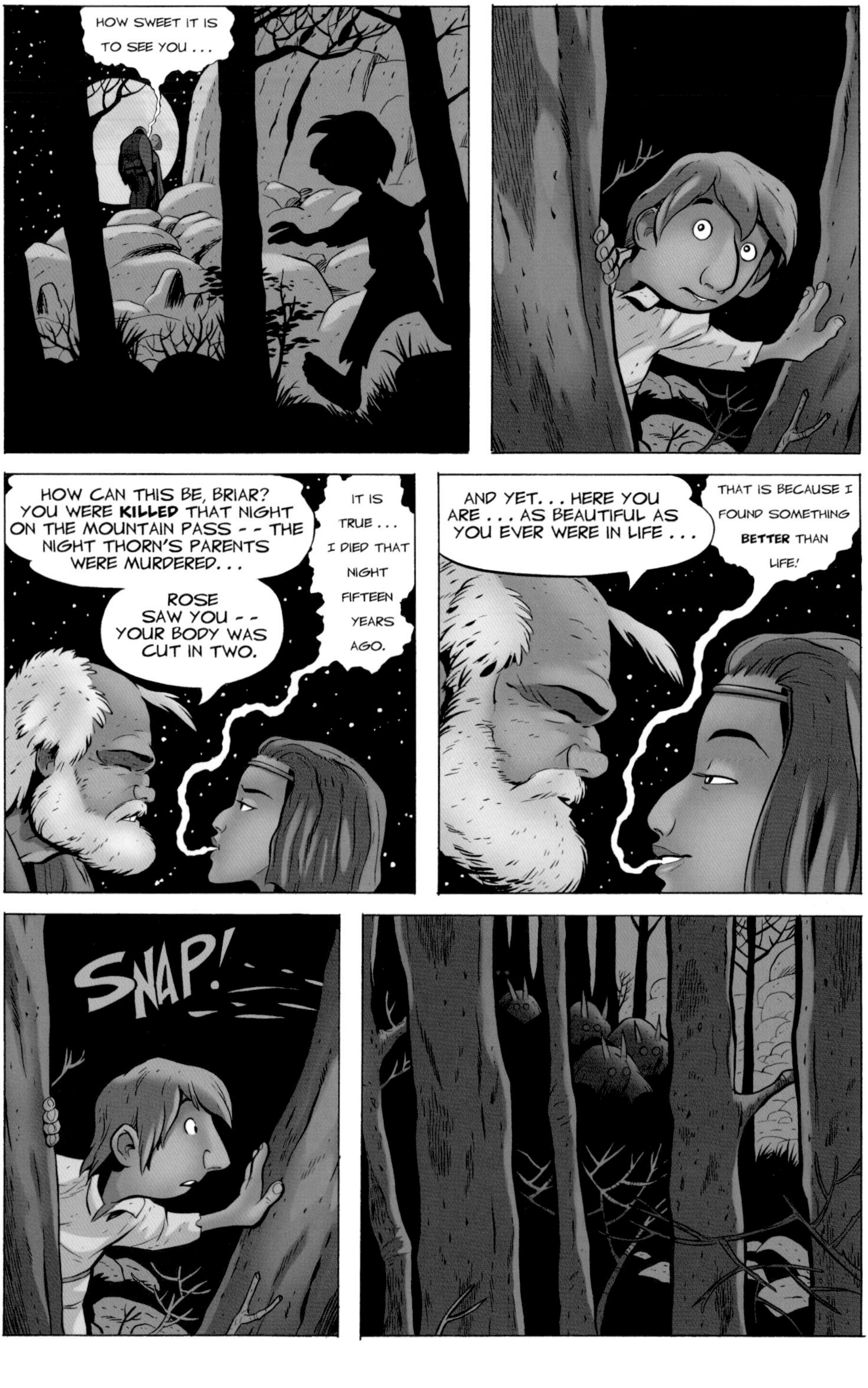
HOW SWEET IT IS TO SEE YOU . . .
HOW CAN THIS BE, BRIAR? YOU WERE **KILLED** THAT NIGHT ON THE MOUNTAIN PASS - - THE NIGHT THORN'S PARENTS WERE MURDERED. . .
ROSE SAW YOU - - YOUR BODY WAS CUT IN TWO.
IT IS TRUE . . . I DIED THAT NIGHT FIFTEEN YEARS AGO.
AND YET. . . HERE YOU ARE . . . AS BEAUTIFUL AS YOU EVER WERE IN LIFE . . .
THAT IS BECAUSE I FOUND SOMETHING **BETTER** THAN LIFE!
SNAP!

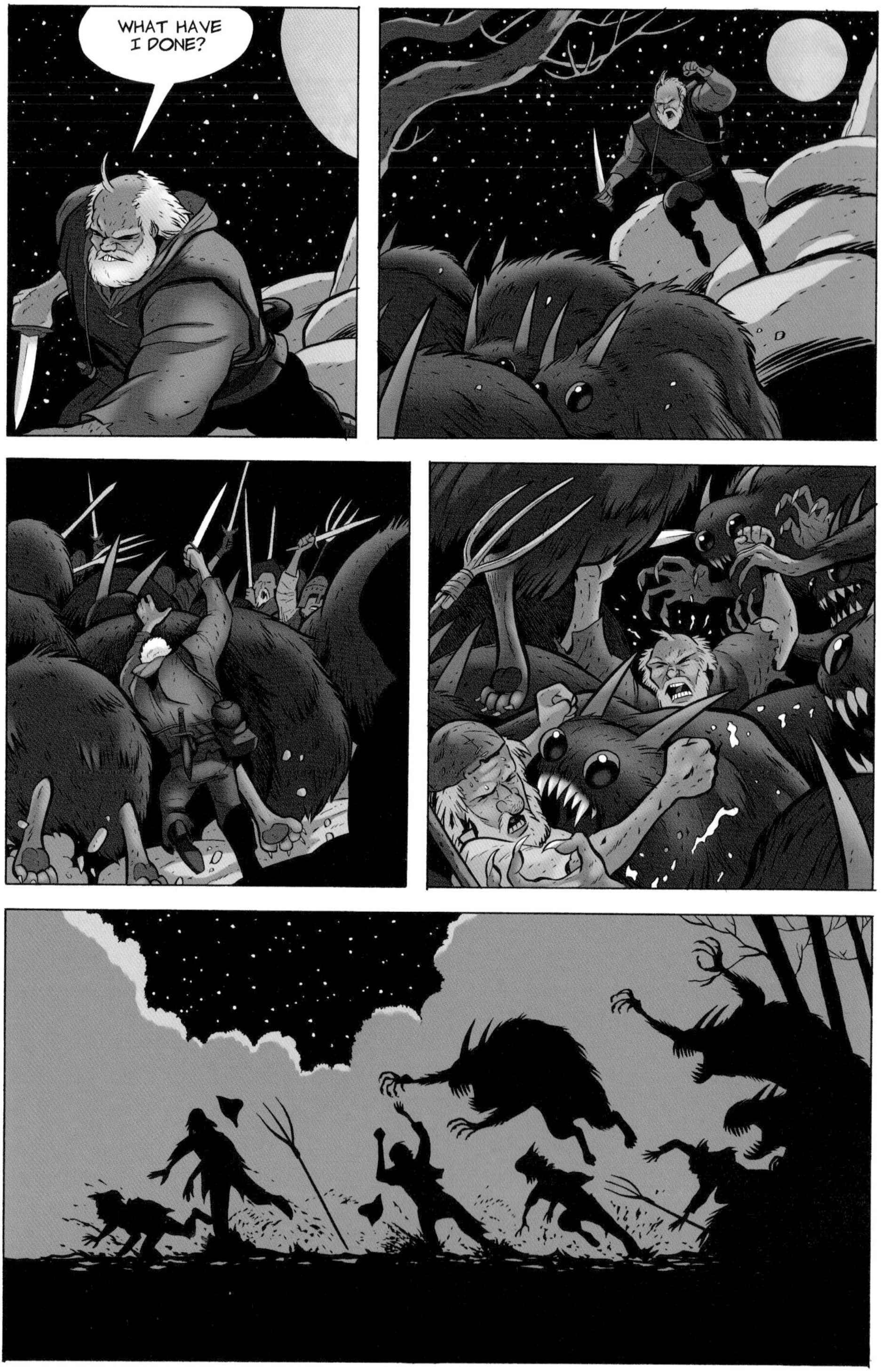
WHAT HAVE I DONE?

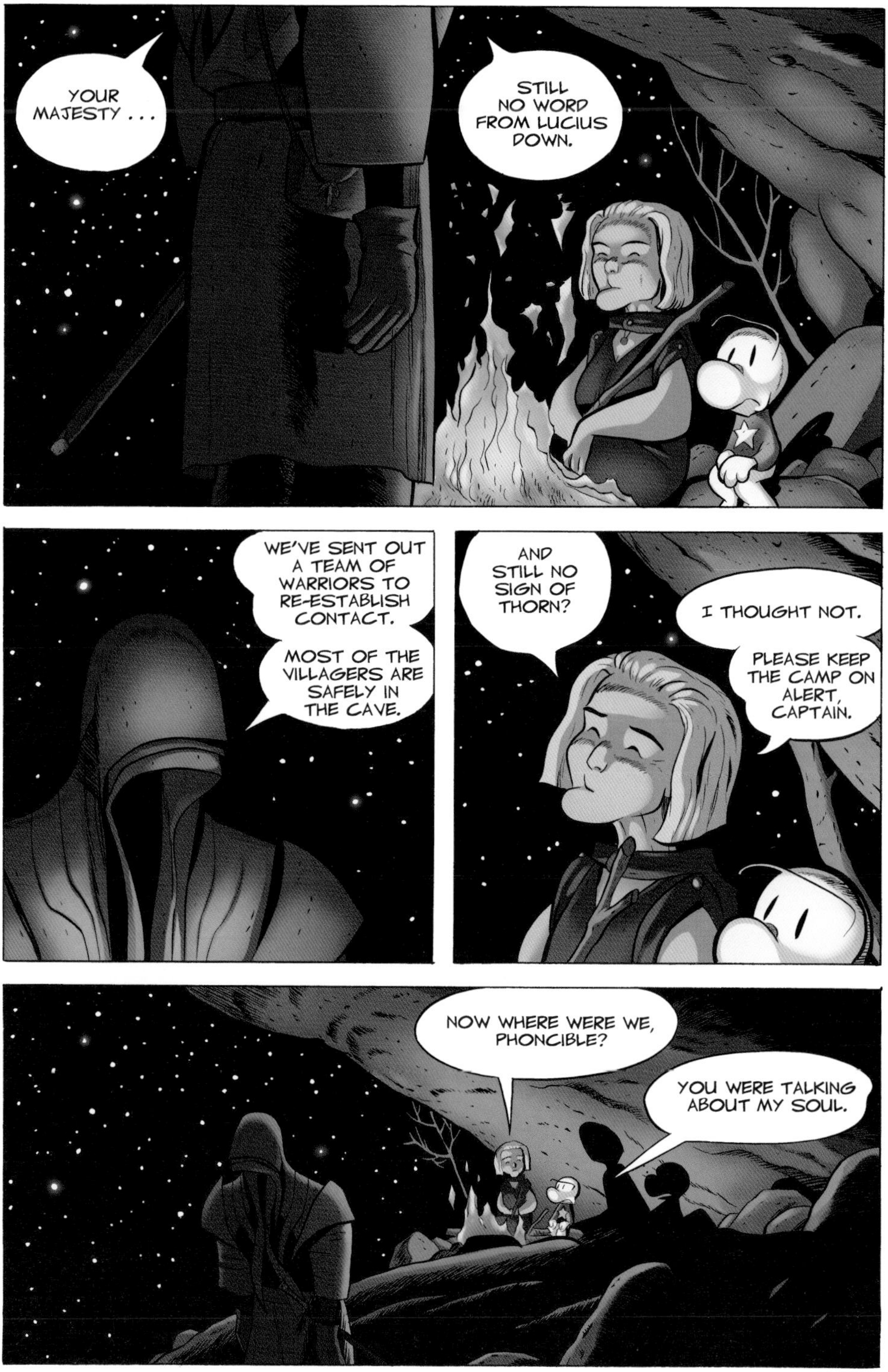
YOUR MAJESTY . . .
STILL NO WORD FROM LUCIUS DOWN.
WE'VE SENT OUT A TEAM OF WARRIORS TO RE-ESTABLISH CONTACT.
MOST OF THE VILLAGERS ARE SAFELY IN THE CAVE.
AND STILL NO SIGN OF THORN?
I THOUGHT NOT.
PLEASE KEEP THE CAMP ON ALERT, CAPTAIN.
NOW WHERE WERE WE, PHONCIBLE?
YOU WERE TALKING ABOUT MY SOUL.

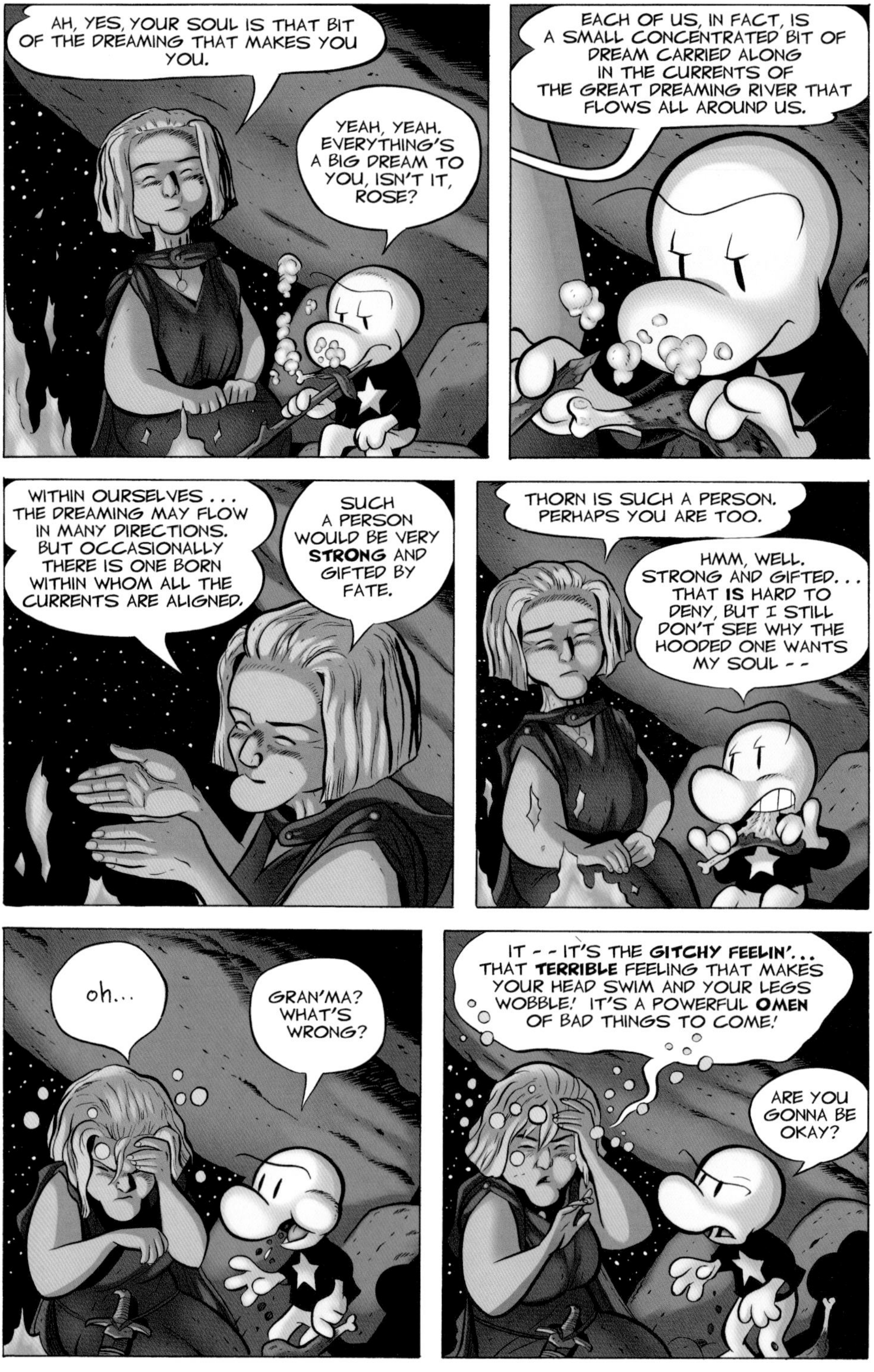
AH, YES, YOUR SOUL IS THAT BIT OF THE DREAMING THAT MAKES YOU YOU.
YEAH, YEAH. EVERYTHING'S A BIG DREAM TO YOU, ISN'T IT, ROSE?
EACH OF US, IN FACT, IS A SMALL CONCENTRATED BIT OF DREAM CARRIED ALONG IN THE CURRENTS OF THE GREAT DREAMING RIVER THAT FLOWS ALL AROUND US.
WITHIN OURSELVES . . . THE DREAMING MAY FLOW IN MANY DIRECTIONS. BUT OCCASIONALLY THERE IS ONE BORN WITHIN WHOM ALL THE CURRENTS ARE ALIGNED.
SUCH A PERSON WOULD BE VERY STRONG AND GIFTED BY FATE.
THORN IS SUCH A PERSON. PERHAPS YOU ARE TOO.
HMM, WELL. STRONG AND GIFTED. . . THAT IS HARD TO DENY, BUT I STILL DON'T SEE WHY THE HOODED ONE WANTS MY SOUL - -
oh...
GRAN'MA? WHAT'S WRONG?
IT - - IT'S THE GITCHY FEELIN'. . . THAT TERRIBLE FEELING THAT MAKES YOUR HEAD SWIM AND YOUR LEGS WOBBLE! IT'S A POWERFUL OMEN OF BAD THINGS TO COME!
ARE YOU GONNA BE OKAY?

YES, I . . . I JUST HOPE THAT MY GRANDDAUGHTER IS SAFE . . . .

?

HEY-- YOU FEEL THAT?

RRRRUMB!

CRACK!

RUMMBLE

SMASH!

IT'S AN EARTHQUAKE! GET OUTSIDE!

IS IT OVER?

WHAT HAPPENED?

YOUR MAJESTY! **LOOK!** LOOK AT THE EASTERN MOUNTAINS!

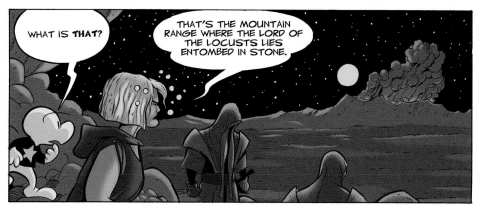

WHAT IS **THAT?**

THAT'S THE MOUNTAIN RANGE WHERE THE LORD OF THE LOCUSTS LIES ENTOMBED IN STONE.

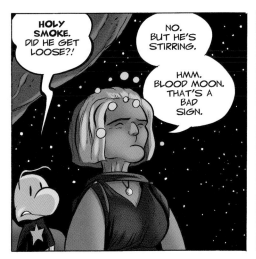

HOLY SMOKE. DID HE GET LOOSE?!

NO. BUT HE'S STIRRING.

HMM. BLOOD MOON. THAT'S A BAD SIGN.

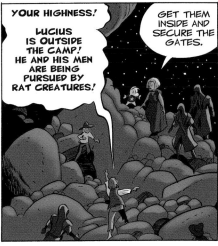

YOUR HIGHNESS! LUCIUS IS OUTSIDE THE CAMP! HE AND HIS MEN ARE BEING PURSUED BY RAT CREATURES!

GET THEM INSIDE AND SECURE THE GATES.

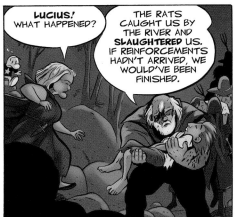

LUCIUS! WHAT HAPPENED?

THE RATS CAUGHT US BY THE RIVER AND **SLAUGHTERED** US. IF REINFORCEMENTS HADN'T ARRIVED, WE WOULD'VE BEEN FINISHED.

I SHOULD HAVE BEEN WITH YOU.

I WISH YOU HAD BEEN . . .

HERE. TAKE HIM. I DON'T KNOW IF HE'S STILL ALIVE OR NOT.

IT'S ALL MY FAULT, ROSE.

THE RAT CREATURES HAVE US COMPLETELY SURROUNDED.

CALM. BE CALM. WE MUST PREPARE FOR OUR FINAL STAND.

I JUST PRAY THAT THORN IS SAFE . . . WHEREVER SHE IS.

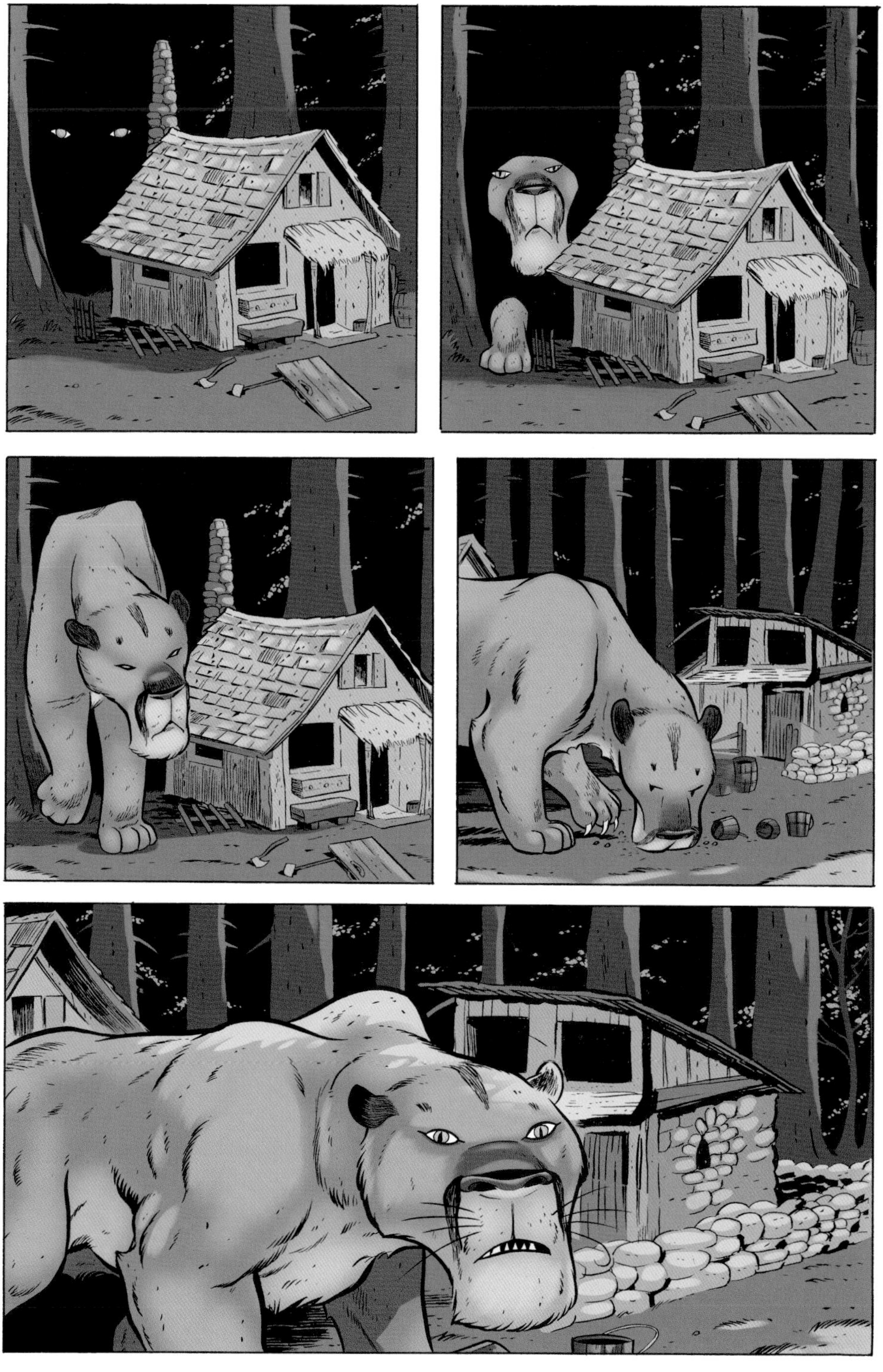

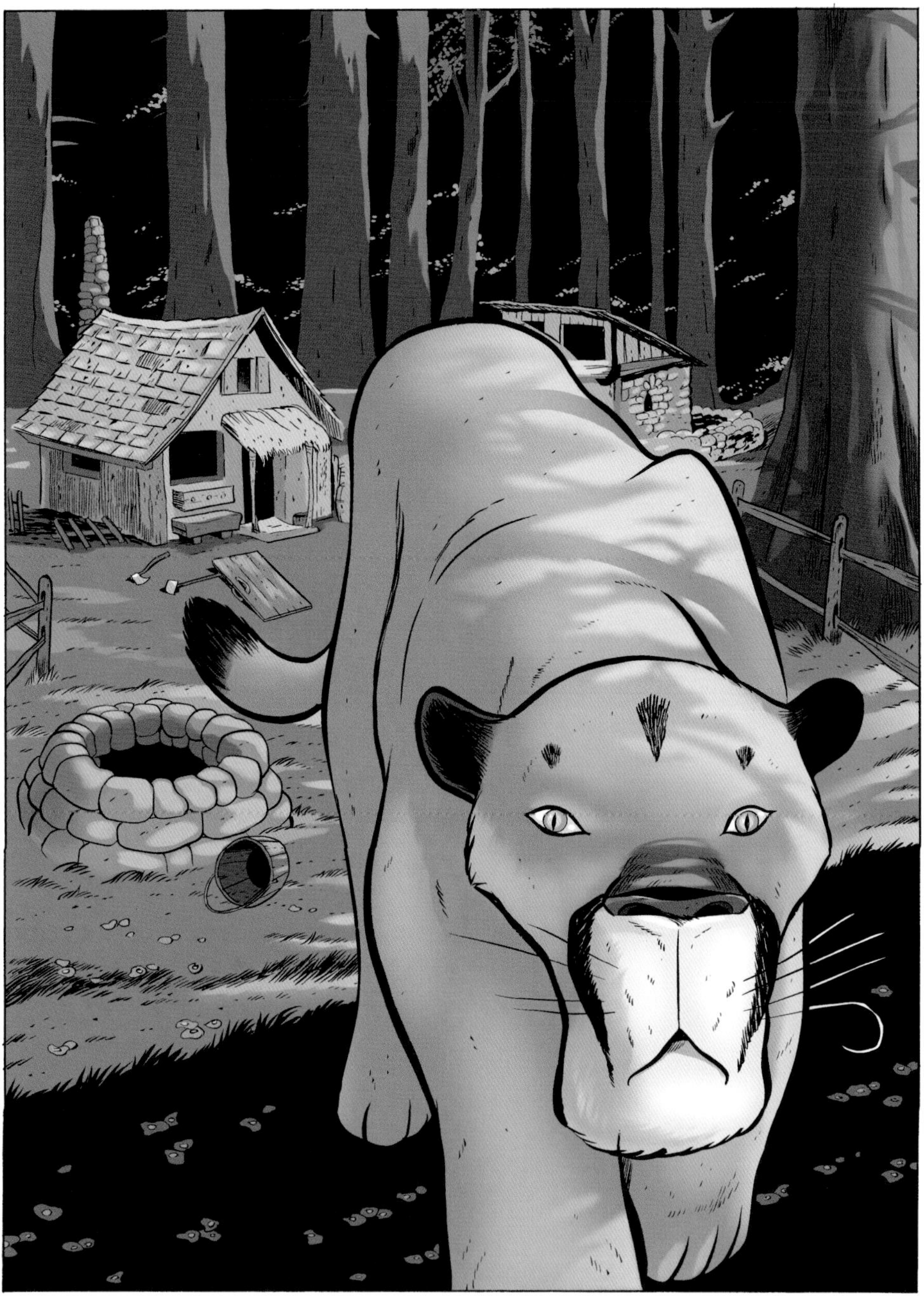

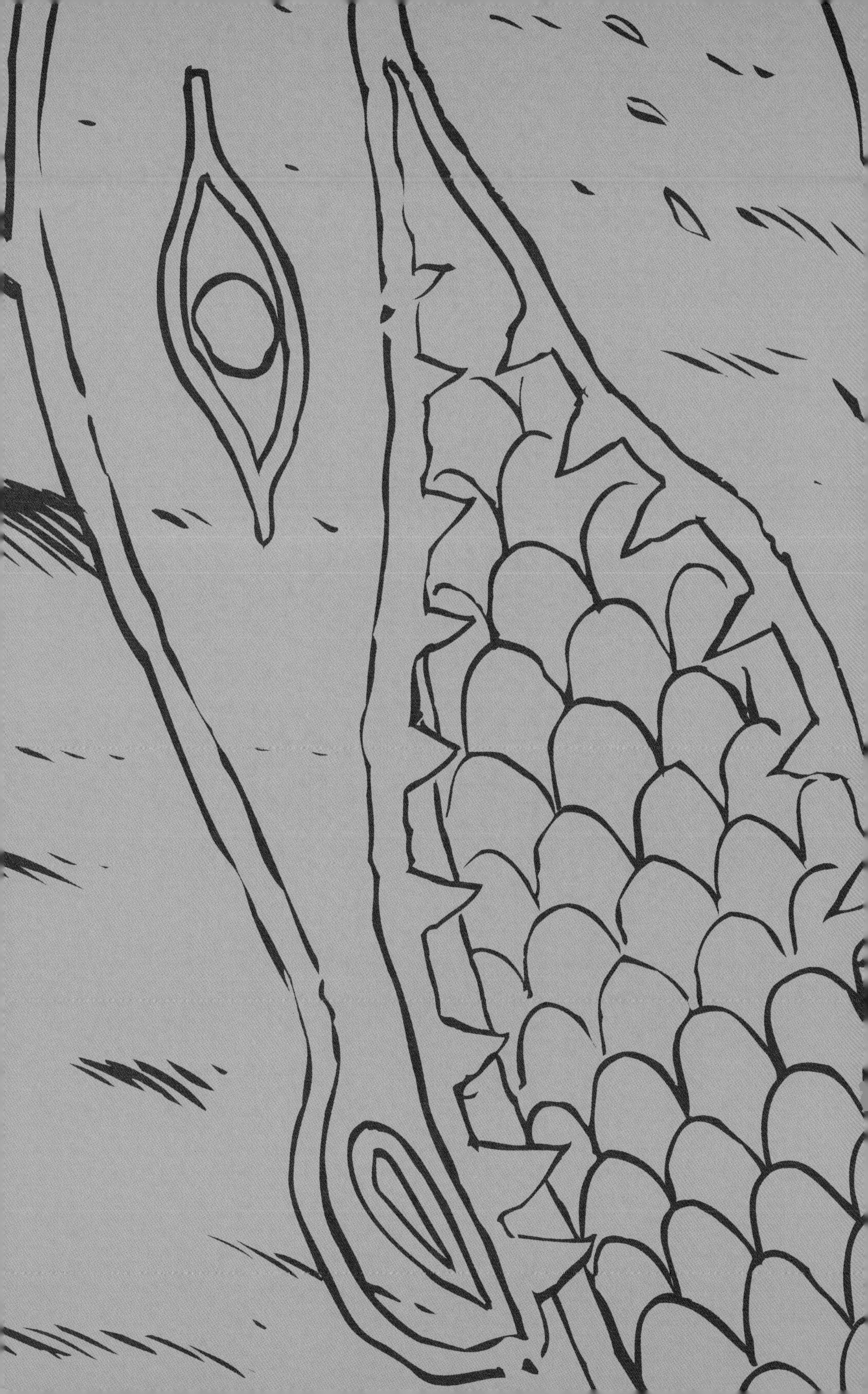

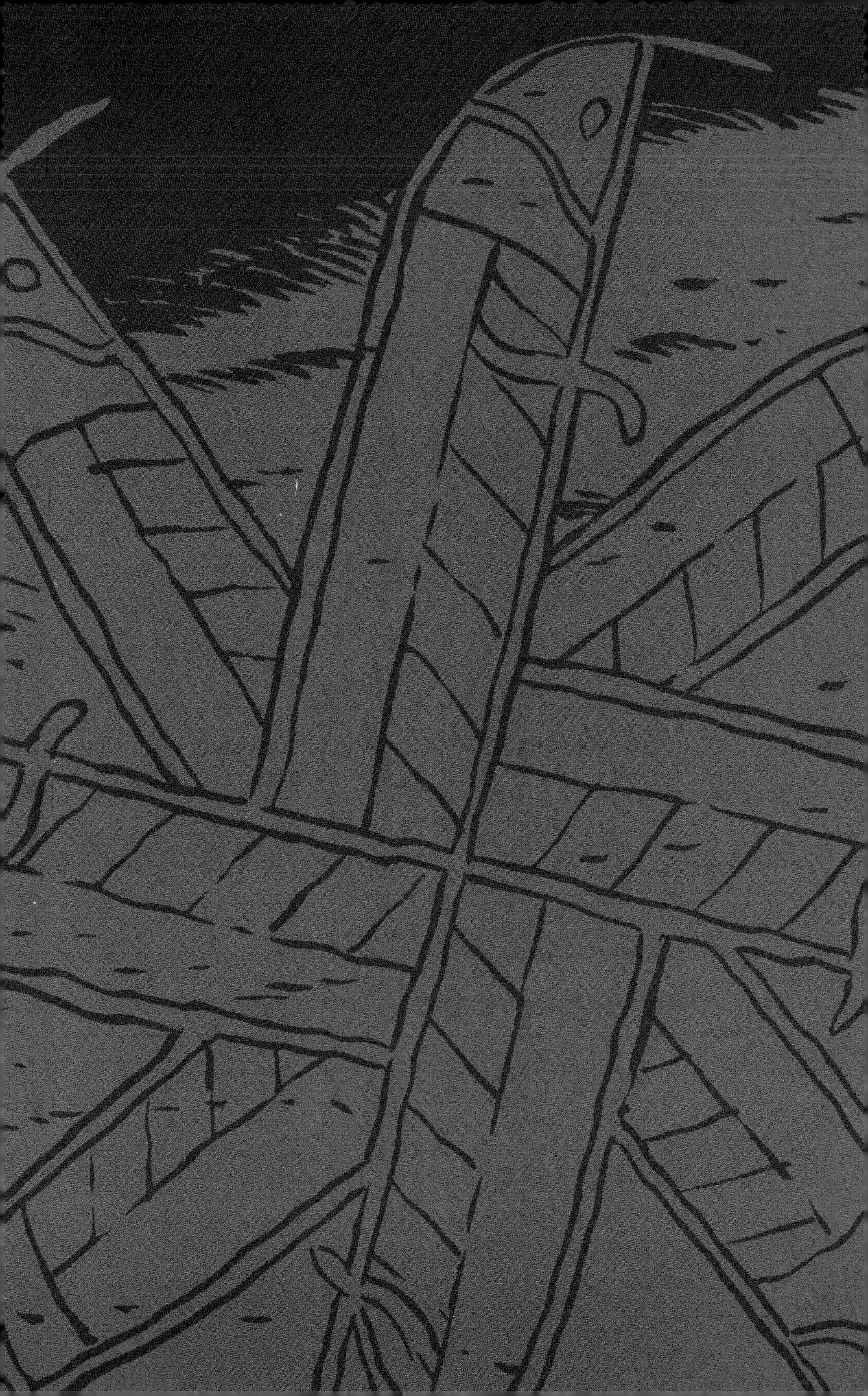

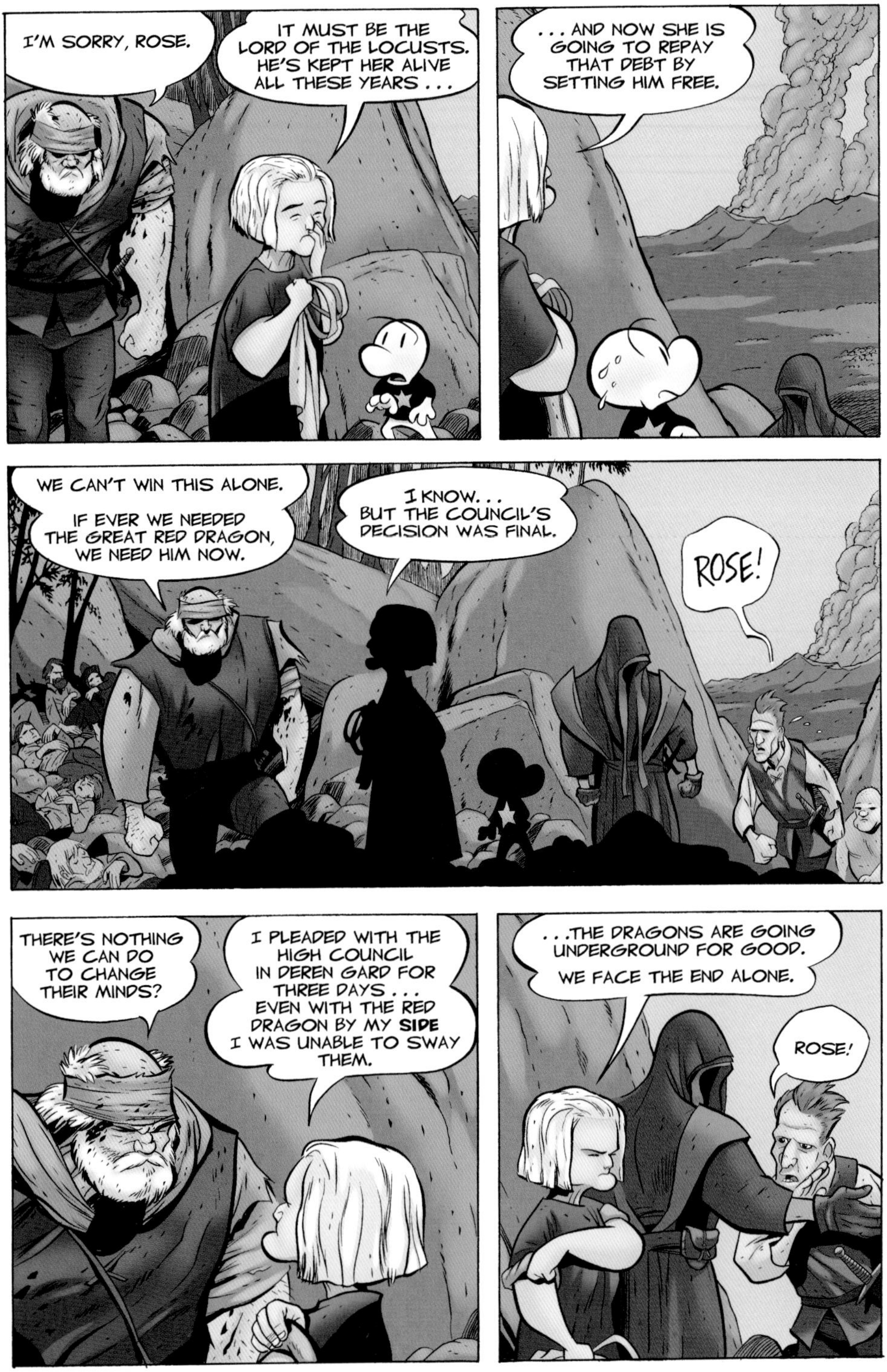
I'M SORRY, ROSE.
IT MUST BE THE LORD OF THE LOCUSTS. HE'S KEPT HER ALIVE ALL THESE YEARS . . .
. . . AND NOW SHE IS GOING TO REPAY THAT DEBT BY SETTING HIM FREE.
WE CAN'T WIN THIS ALONE.
IF EVER WE NEEDED THE GREAT RED DRAGON, WE NEED HIM NOW.
I KNOW. . . BUT THE COUNCIL'S DECISION WAS FINAL.
ROSE!
THERE'S NOTHING WE CAN DO TO CHANGE THEIR MINDS?
I PLEADED WITH THE HIGH COUNCIL IN DEREN GARD FOR THREE DAYS . . . EVEN WITH THE RED DRAGON BY MY **SIDE** I WAS UNABLE TO SWAY THEM.
. . .THE DRAGONS ARE GOING UNDERGROUND FOR GOOD.
WE FACE THE END ALONE.
ROSE!

IT'S ALL RIGHT, CAPTAIN. WHAT IS IT, WENDELL?

GIVE **HIM** TO US, ROSE!

YEAH! THIS IS ALL **HIS** FAULT!

WHOSE FAULT, DEAR?

PHONEY BONE! "THE ONE WHO BEARS THE STAR."

HE'S THE ONE THE RAT CREATURES ARE AFTER. THEY TORE UP THE VALLEY LOOKING FOR HIM.

YEAH! NOW THE RAT CREATURES HAVE US SURROUNDED! IF **HE'S** ALL THEY WANT, LET'S HAND HIM OVER!

EVEN IF HE **WAS** ALL THE RAT CREATURES WANTED, I WOULDN'T ADVISE GIVING THEM THE ONE THING THEY NEED TO WIN THIS WAR.

WHAT DO YOU MEAN?

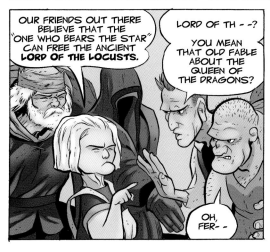

OUR FRIENDS OUT THERE BELIEVE THAT THE "ONE WHO BEARS THE STAR" CAN FREE THE ANCIENT **LORD OF THE LOCUSTS.**

LORD OF TH--?

YOU MEAN THAT OLD FABLE ABOUT THE QUEEN OF THE DRAGONS?

OH, FER--

--THAT'S JUST A **STORY!** GIVE THEM PHONEY BONE AND LET 'EM TRY! WHAT CAN THE LORD OF THE LOCUSTS DO TO **US?**

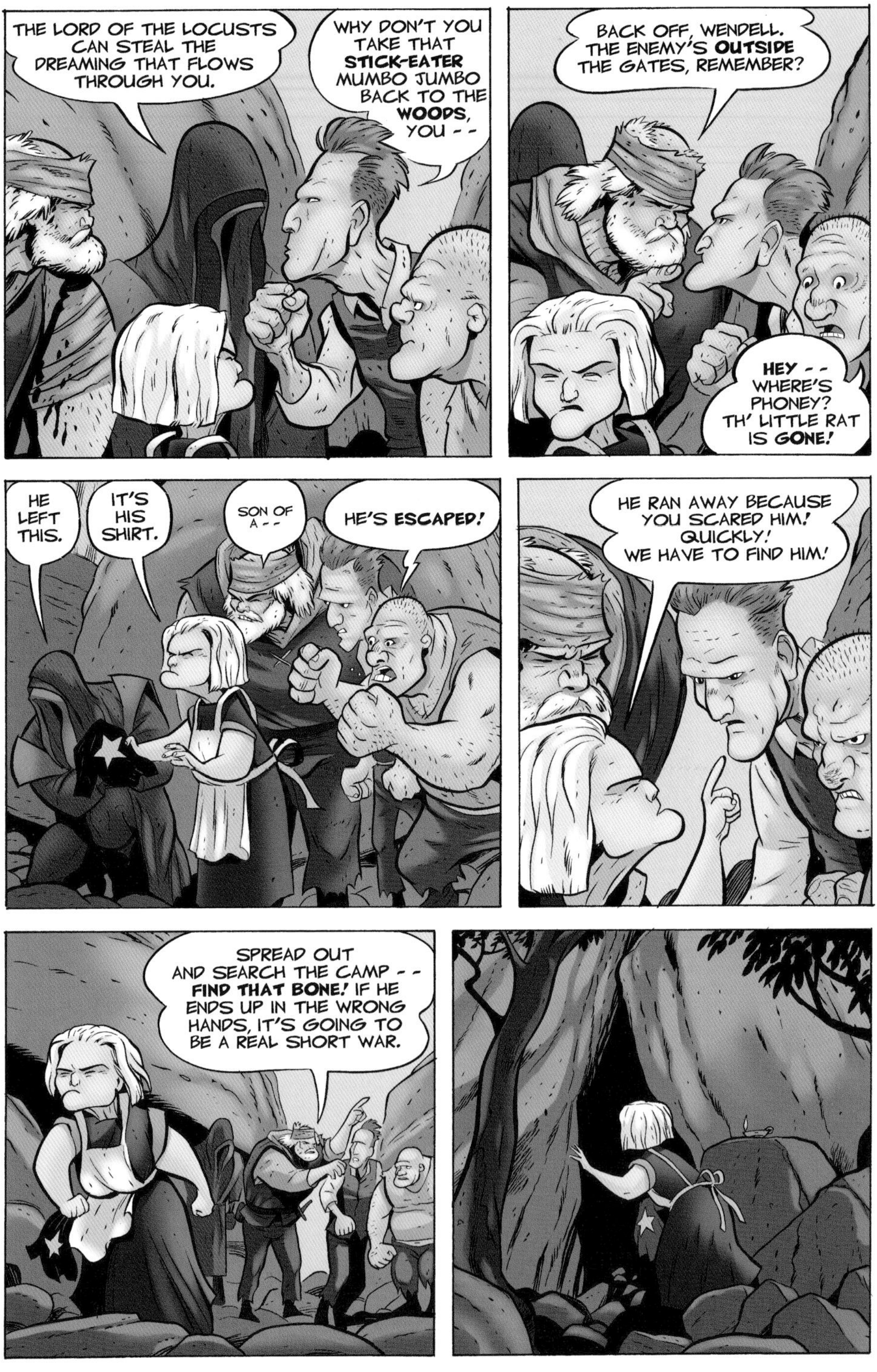
THE LORD OF THE LOCUSTS CAN STEAL THE DREAMING THAT FLOWS THROUGH YOU.
WHY DON'T YOU TAKE THAT STICK-EATER MUMBO JUMBO BACK TO THE WOODS, YOU - -
BACK OFF, WENDELL. THE ENEMY'S OUTSIDE THE GATES, REMEMBER?
HEY - - WHERE'S PHONEY? TH' LITTLE RAT IS GONE!
HE LEFT THIS.
IT'S HIS SHIRT.
SON OF A - -
HE'S ESCAPED!
HE RAN AWAY BECAUSE YOU SCARED HIM! QUICKLY! WE HAVE TO FIND HIM!
SPREAD OUT AND SEARCH THE CAMP - - FIND THAT BONE! IF HE ENDS UP IN THE WRONG HANDS, IT'S GOING TO BE A REAL SHORT WAR.

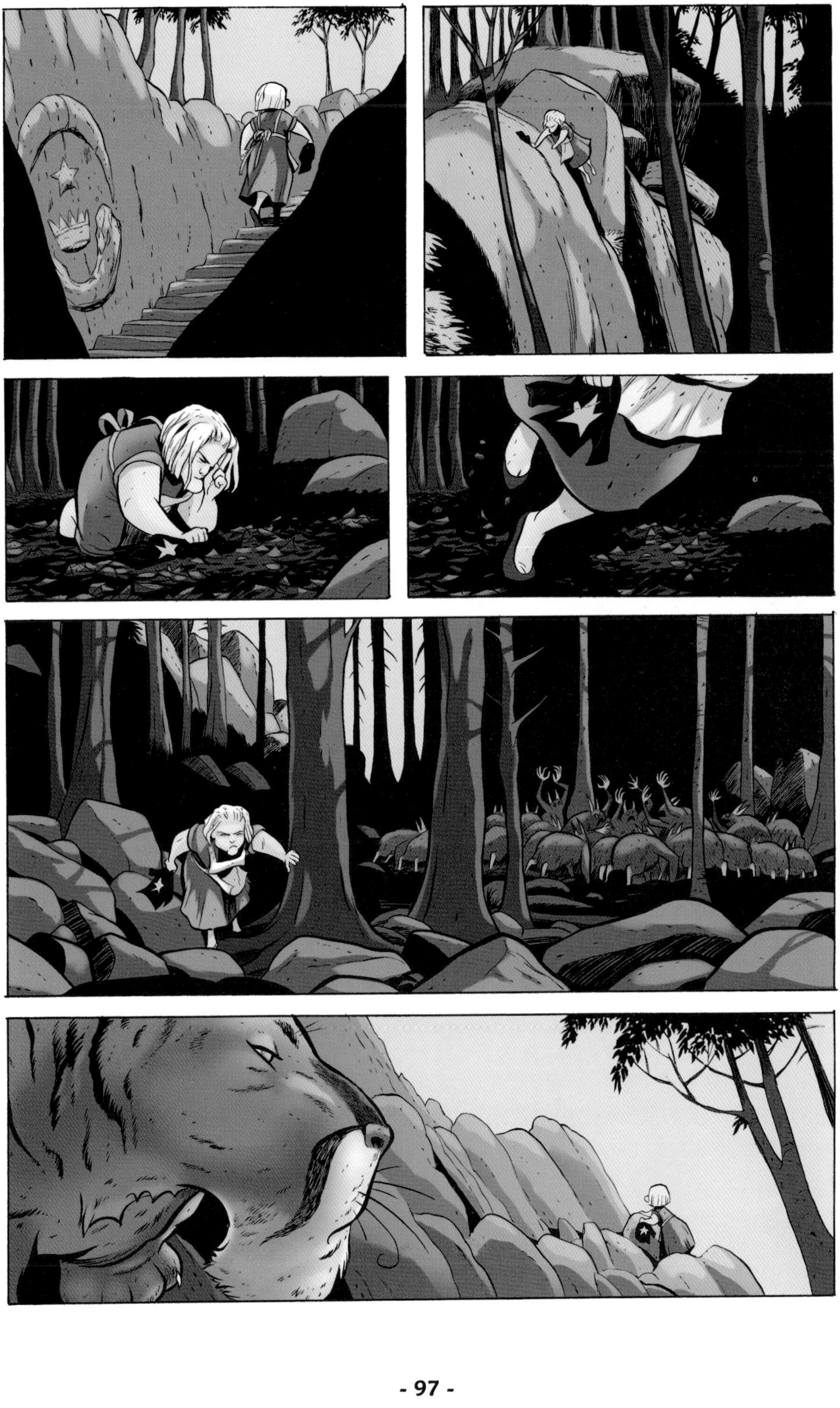

HOLD IT RIGHT THERE, SQUIRT!

GRAN'MA --

WHERE DO YOU THINK **YOU'RE** GOING?

I HAD TO RUN AWAY...

HAVEN'T YOU CAUSED ENOUGH TROUBLE?

EVERYONE WAS IN **DANGER** AS LONG AS I STAYED THERE...

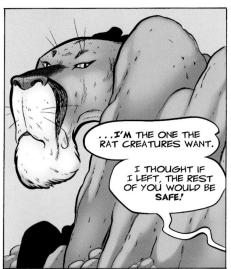

...I'M THE ONE THE RAT CREATURES WANT.

I THOUGHT IF I LEFT, THE REST OF YOU WOULD BE **SAFE!**

HORSE KNOBBIES!! YOU DON'T CARE ABOUT ANYBODY'S **SAFETY!** YOU WERE RUNNING AWAY...

BLOOD MOON

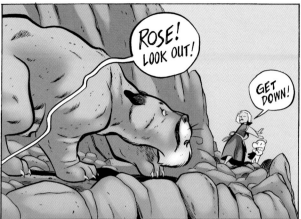

FONE BONE!

PHONEY! WHAT ARE YOU DOING HERE?

AND WHY ARE YOU **NAKED?**

YOU GUYS GOTTA GET **AWAY** FROM ME! EVERYBODY'S AFTER ME BECAUSE I WEAR A **STAR** ON MY SHIRT!

COME WITH US, PHONEY, WE'RE GOING TO OLD MAN'S CAVE. YOU'LL BE SAFE THERE.

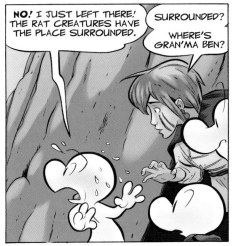

NO! I JUST LEFT THERE! THE RAT CREATURES HAVE THE PLACE SURROUNDED.

SURROUNDED?

WHERE'S GRAN'MA BEN?

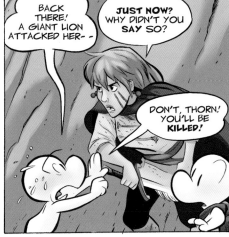

BACK THERE! A GIANT LION ATTACKED HER--

JUST NOW? WHY DIDN'T YOU **SAY** SO?

DON'T, THORN! YOU'LL BE **KILLED!**

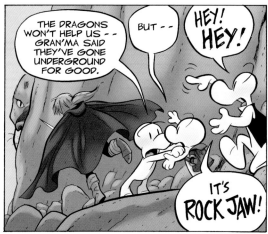

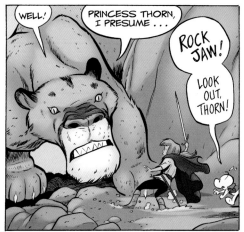

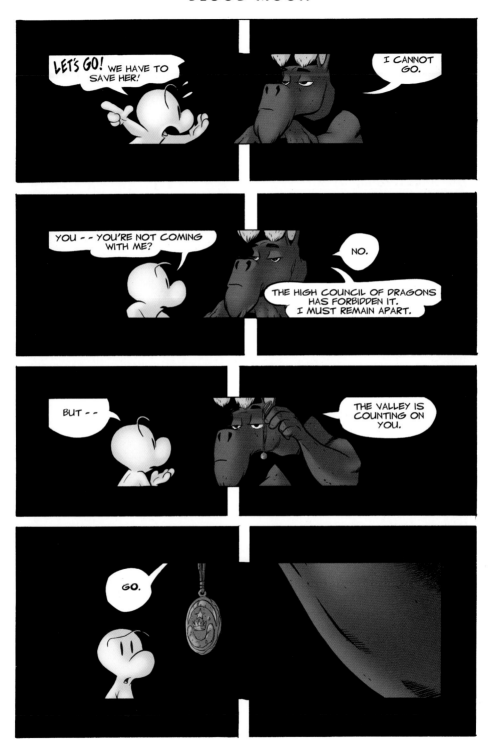

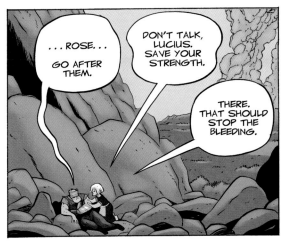

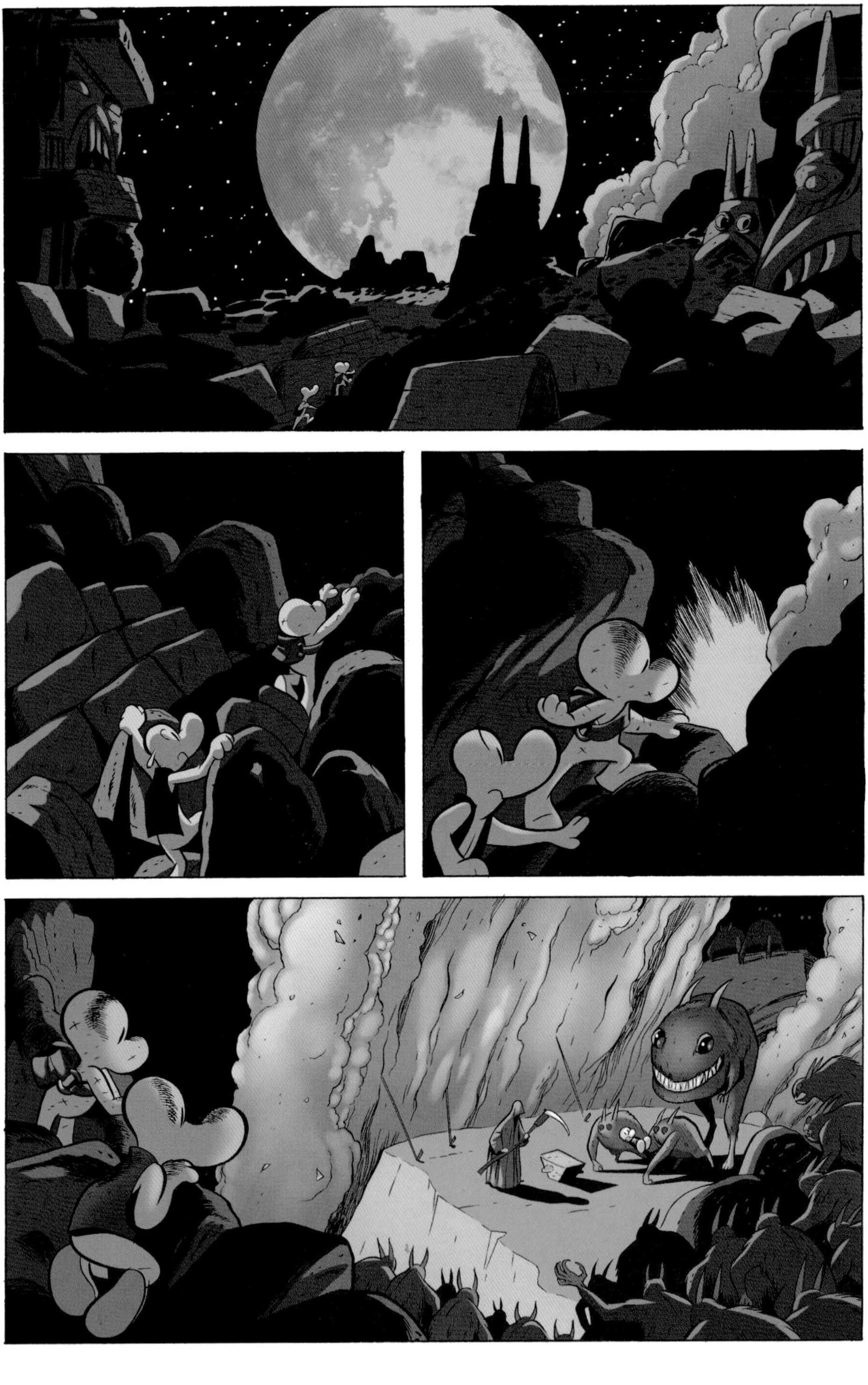

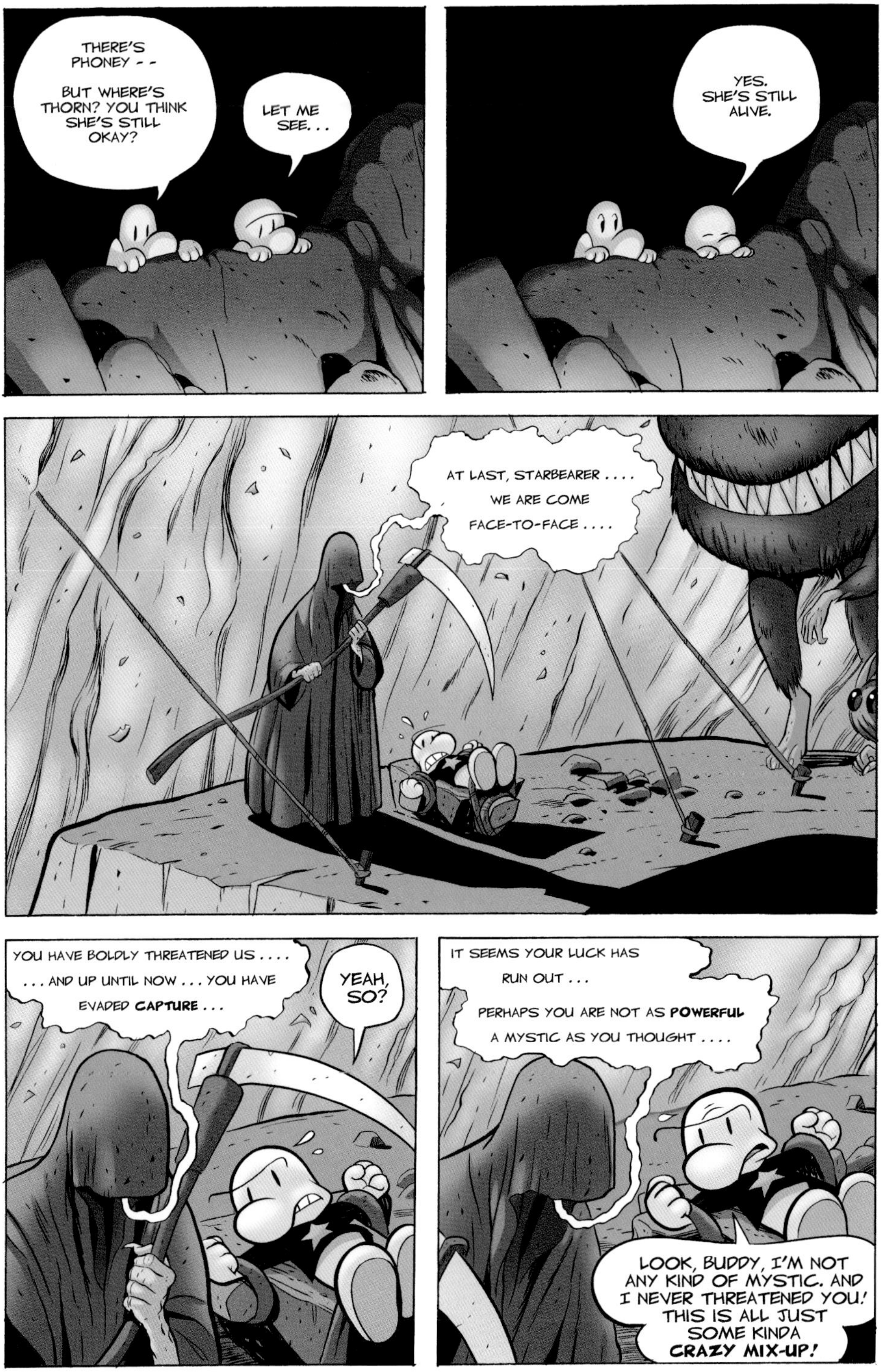
THERE'S PHONEY - - BUT WHERE'S THORN? YOU THINK SHE'S STILL OKAY?
LET ME SEE...
YES. SHE'S STILL ALIVE.
AT LAST, STARBEARER.... WE ARE COME FACE-TO-FACE....
YOU HAVE BOLDLY THREATENED US.... ...AND UP UNTIL NOW...YOU HAVE EVADED **CAPTURE**...
YEAH, SO?
IT SEEMS YOUR LUCK HAS RUN OUT... PERHAPS YOU ARE NOT AS **POWERFUL** A MYSTIC AS YOU THOUGHT....
LOOK, BUDDY, I'M NOT ANY KIND OF MYSTIC. AND I NEVER THREATENED YOU! THIS IS ALL JUST SOME KINDA **CRAZY MIX-UP!**

SILENCE . . .
FROM THIS MOMENT ON YOUR DESTINY IS
WITH ME . . . .
TOGETHER WE WILL **FREE** OUR MASTER
. . . THE ANCIENT **LORD OF**
THE LOCUSTS . . . .

TAKE MY
HAND,
PHONCIBLE P. BONE.
TOUCH ME . . .

FORGET IT!
I AIN'T TAKIN'
YOUR CREEPY
HAND!

THE BLOOD MOON WAXES FULL . . .
THE FORCES OF THE
DREAMING . . . . AND OUR MASTER . . . ARE
BEING DRAWN CLOSER
TO THE STONE SURFACE THAT
SEPARATES US . . .

YOU'RE
NUTS!

IF YOU DO NOT JOIN WITH
ME **WILLINGLY** . . . I AM
PREPARED TO RISK THE RITUAL
OF **SACRIFICE** . . . .

SACRIFICE?
NOW, HOLD ON, PAL.
SERIOUSLY, YOU GOT
THE **WRONG GUY!**
IT'S ALL A
BIG **MISTAKE!**

A . . . MISTAKE . . . ?

A **MISTAKE?**

DO YOU CALL **THIS** . . .
A **MISTAKE?**

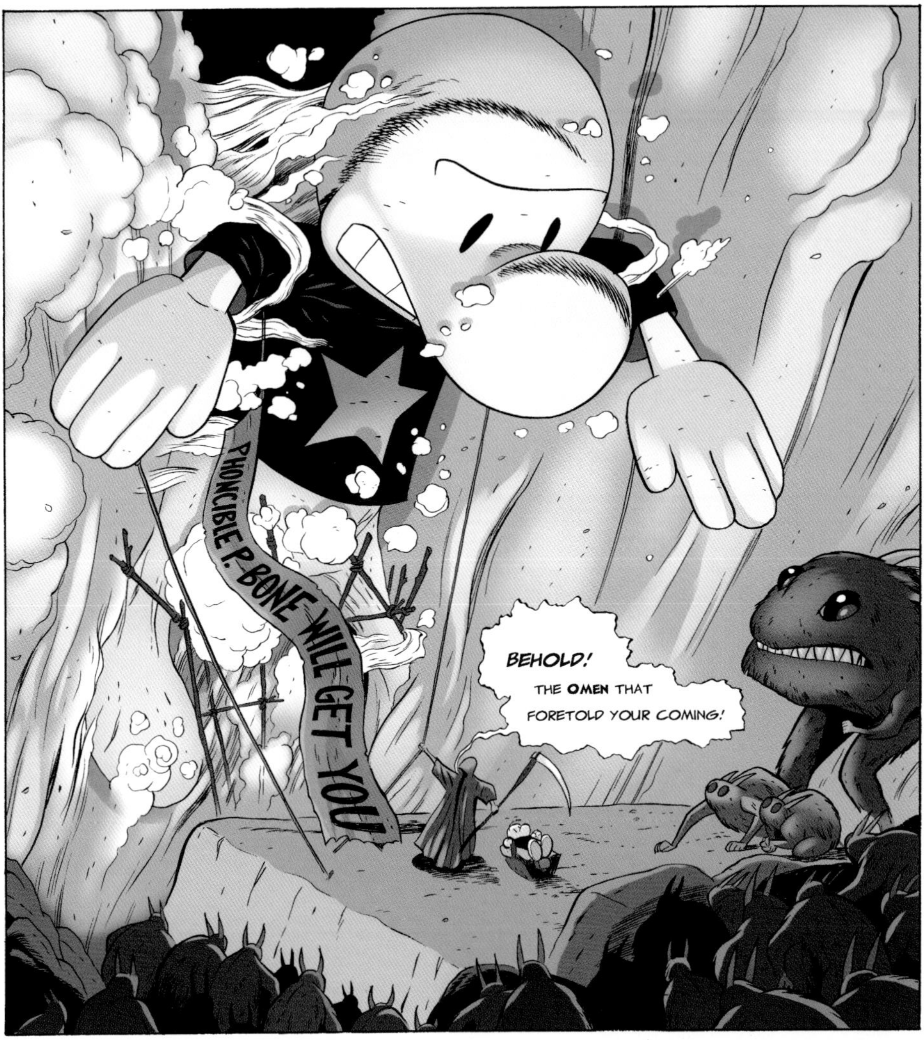
PHONCIBLE P. BONE WILL GET YOU!
BEHOLD! THE OMEN THAT FORETOLD YOUR COMING!

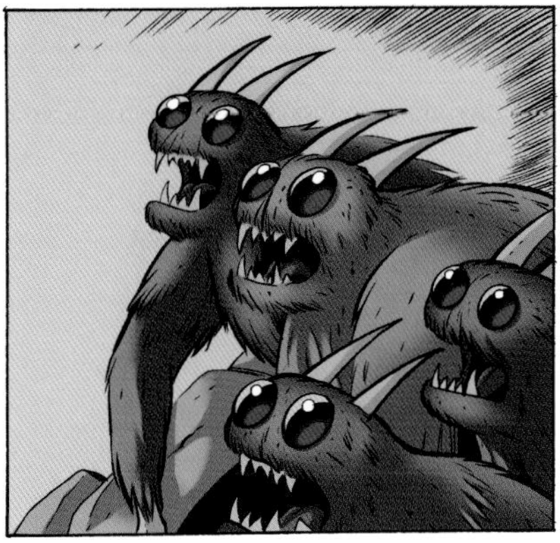

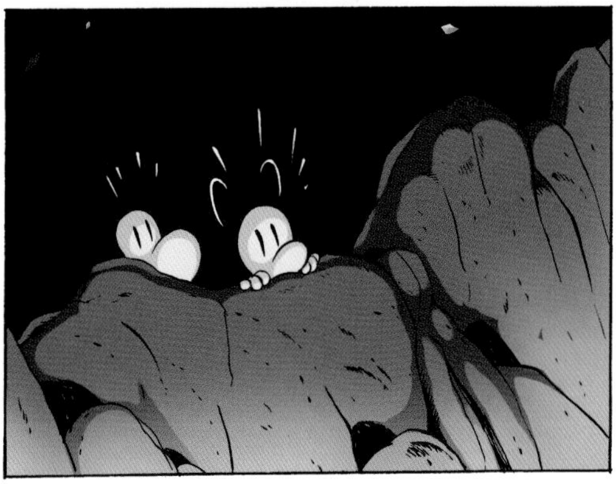

YOU CHASED ME ALL OVER KINGDOM COME BECAUSE OF **THAT?!**.

O BOY. FONE BONE IS GONNA BE CRANKY WHEN HE FINDS OUT ABOUT THIS.

IT'S PHONEY'S **CAMPAIGN BALLOON!** THE ONE THAT CHASED **MISS CRAB-BONE** INTO THE RIVER!

YEAH! THE SAME BALLOON THAT GOT US RUN OUT OF BONEVILLE IN THE FIRST PLACE.

I THOUGHT YOU CAUGHT IT AND LET THE AIR OUT OF IT!

I THOUGHT **YOU** DID! IT MUST HAVE FLOATED HERE ACROSS THE DESERT.

AS SOON AS WE SAVE HIM FROM THIS SACRIFICE, LET'S **KILL** HIM!

THIS IS WHY YOU'VE BEEN SEARCHING FOR ME?! IT'S A CAMPAIGN BALLOON! THE BANNER USED TO SAY: PHONCIBLE P. BONE WILL GET YOUR **VOTE!**

I WILL NOW USE MY SCYTHE ... TO CONNECT YOUR **SOUL** ... DIRECTLY TO THE LIVING ROCK ...

BRIAR!

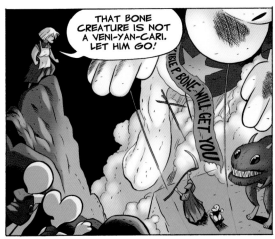

THAT BONE CREATURE IS NOT A VENI-YAN-CARI. LET HIM GO!

'IBLE P. BONE WILL GET YOU

AH, **WELCOME**, ROSE HARVESTAR ... MY **SISTER** ....

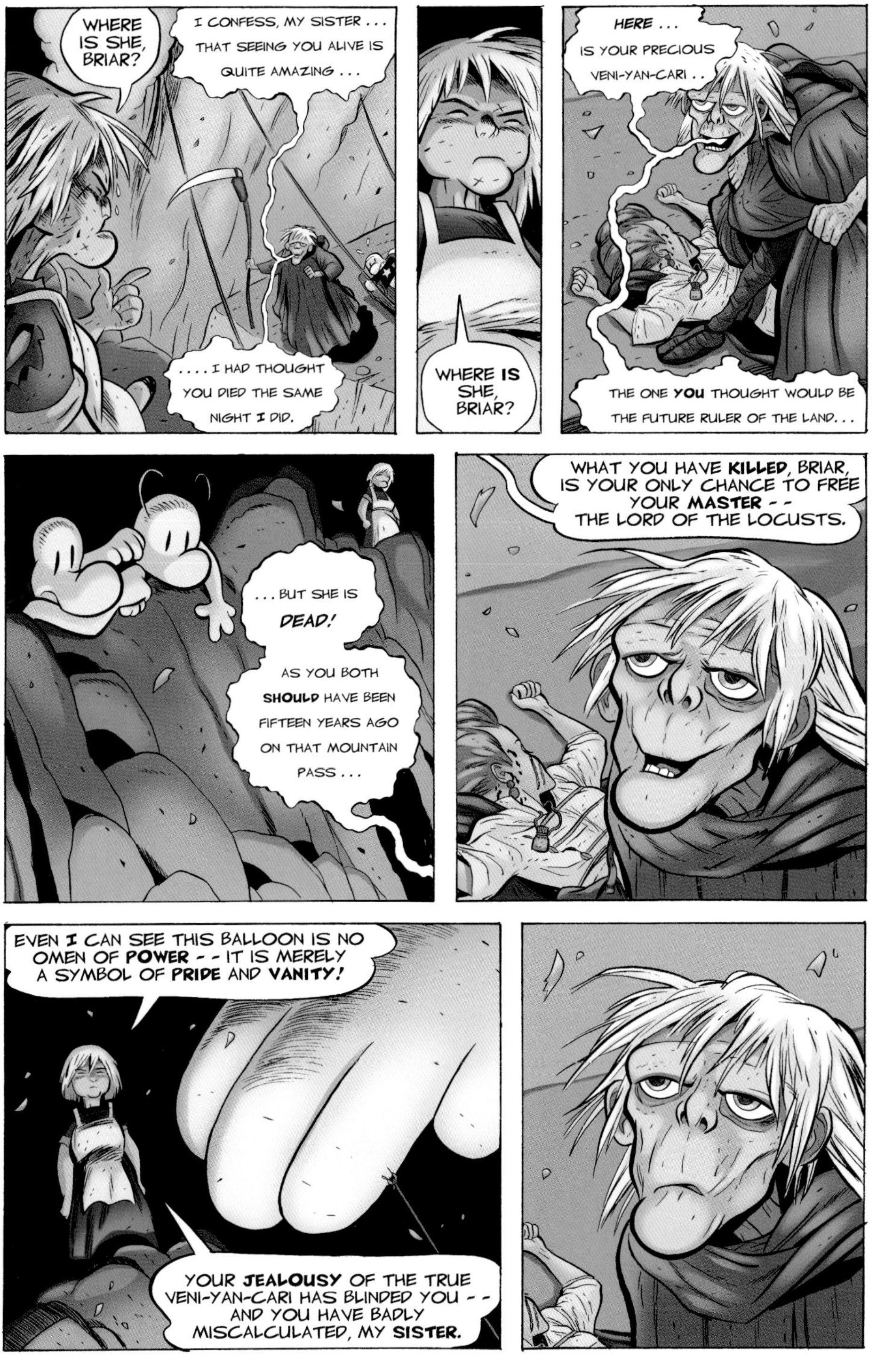
WHERE IS SHE, BRIAR?
I CONFESS, MY SISTER . . . THAT SEEING YOU ALIVE IS QUITE AMAZING . . .
. . . . I HAD THOUGHT YOU DIED THE SAME NIGHT I DID.
WHERE IS SHE, BRIAR?
HERE . . . IS YOUR PRECIOUS VENI-YAN-CARI . .
THE ONE YOU THOUGHT WOULD BE THE FUTURE RULER OF THE LAND. . .
. . . BUT SHE IS DEAD!
AS YOU BOTH SHOULD HAVE BEEN FIFTEEN YEARS AGO ON THAT MOUNTAIN PASS . . .
WHAT YOU HAVE KILLED, BRIAR, IS YOUR ONLY CHANCE TO FREE YOUR MASTER - - THE LORD OF THE LOCUSTS.
EVEN I CAN SEE THIS BALLOON IS NO OMEN OF POWER - - IT IS MERELY A SYMBOL OF PRIDE AND VANITY!
YOUR JEALOUSY OF THE TRUE VENI-YAN-CARI HAS BLINDED YOU - - AND YOU HAVE BADLY MISCALCULATED, MY SISTER.

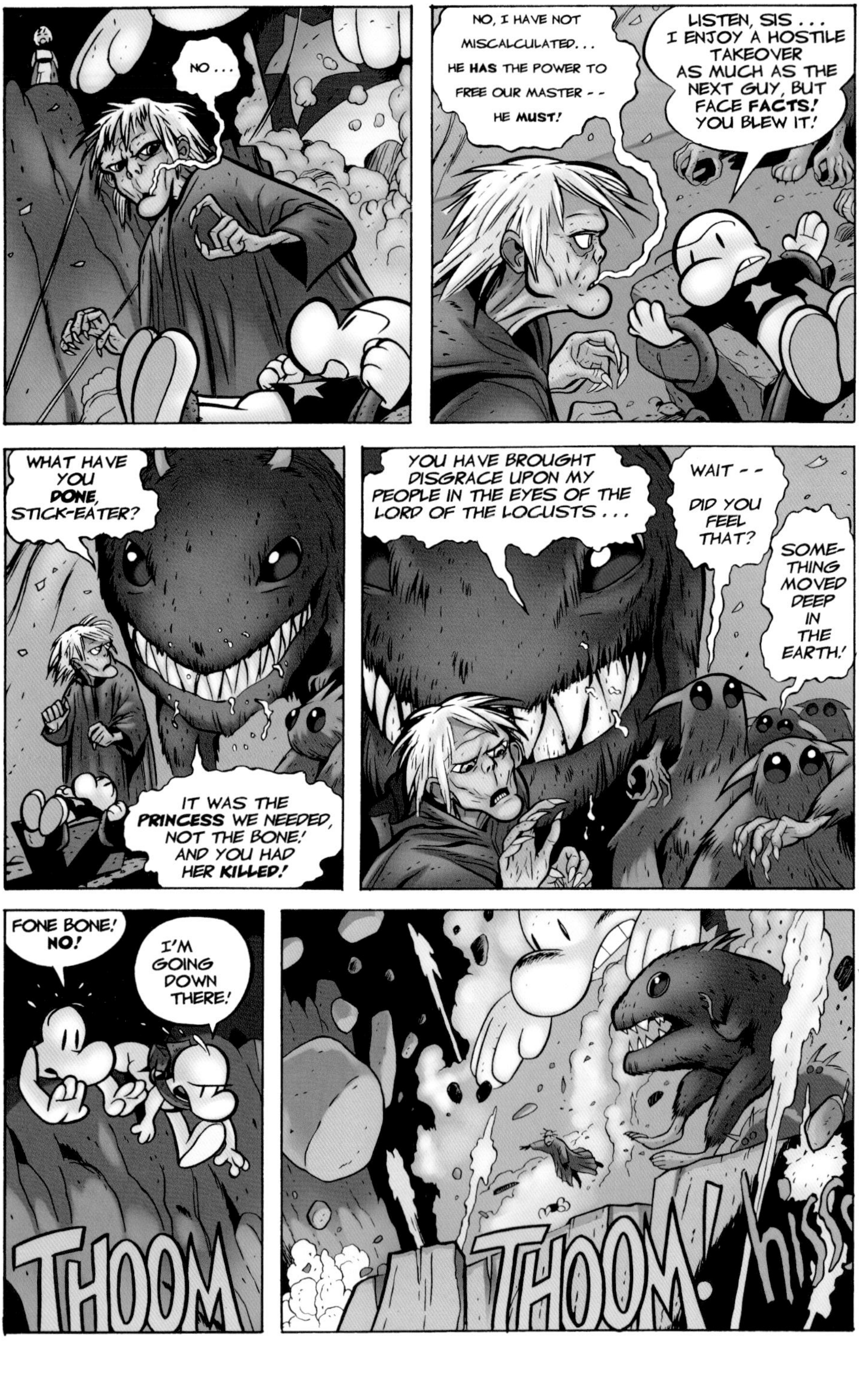
NO . . .
NO, I HAVE NOT MISCALCULATED . . . HE **HAS** THE POWER TO FREE OUR MASTER - - HE **MUST!**
LISTEN, SIS . . . I ENJOY A HOSTILE TAKEOVER AS MUCH AS THE NEXT GUY, BUT FACE **FACTS!** YOU BLEW IT!
WHAT HAVE YOU **DONE**, STICK-EATER?
IT WAS THE **PRINCESS** WE NEEDED, NOT THE BONE! AND YOU HAD HER **KILLED!**
YOU HAVE BROUGHT DISGRACE UPON MY PEOPLE IN THE EYES OF THE LORD OF THE LOCUSTS . . .
WAIT - -
DID YOU FEEL THAT?
SOME-THING MOVED DEEP IN THE EARTH!
FONE BONE! **NO!**
I'M GOING DOWN THERE!
THOOM
THOOM! hiss

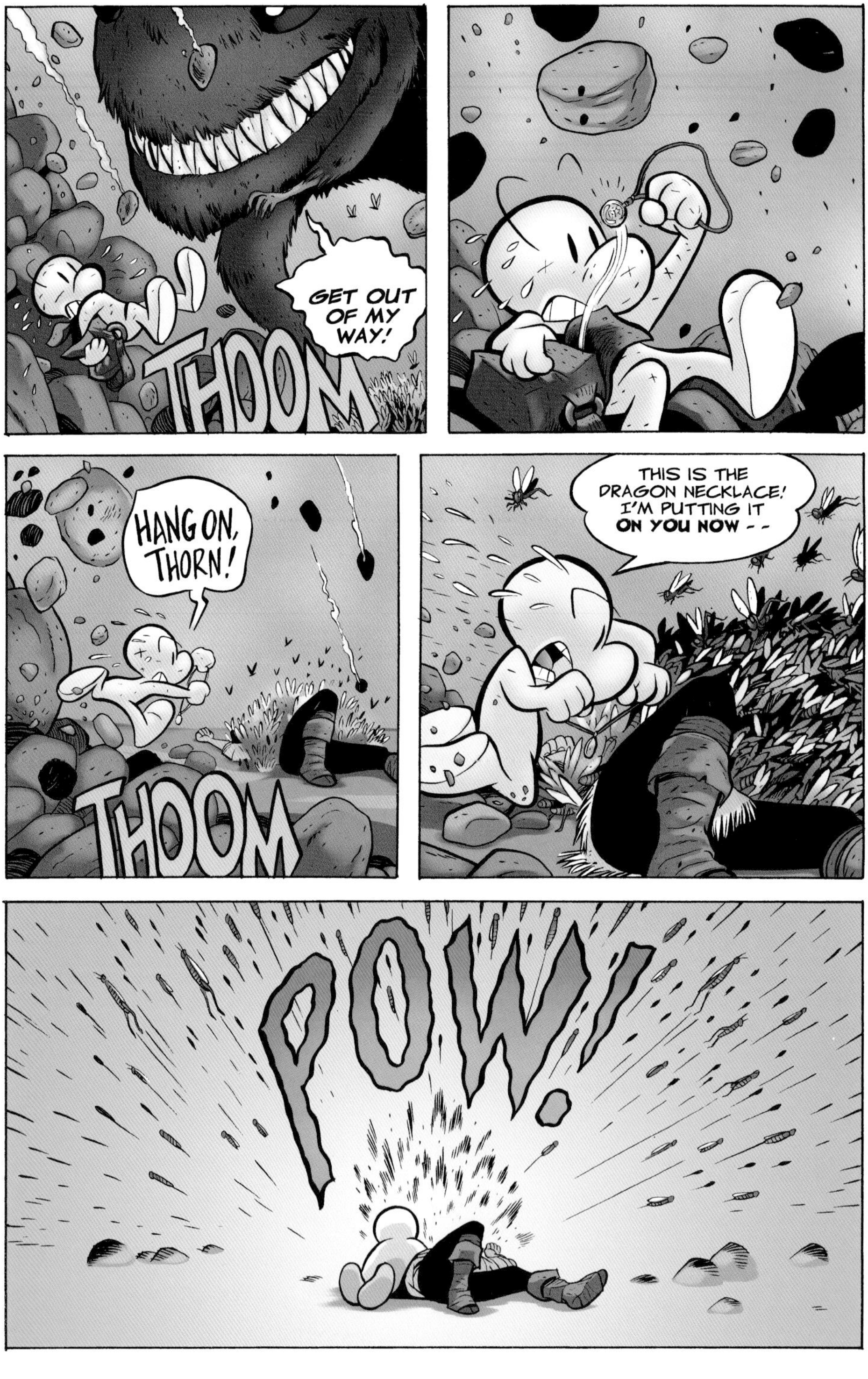
GET OUT OF MY WAY!
THOOM
HANG ON, THORN!
THOOM
THIS IS THE DRAGON NECKLACE! I'M PUTTING IT ON YOU NOW - -
POW!

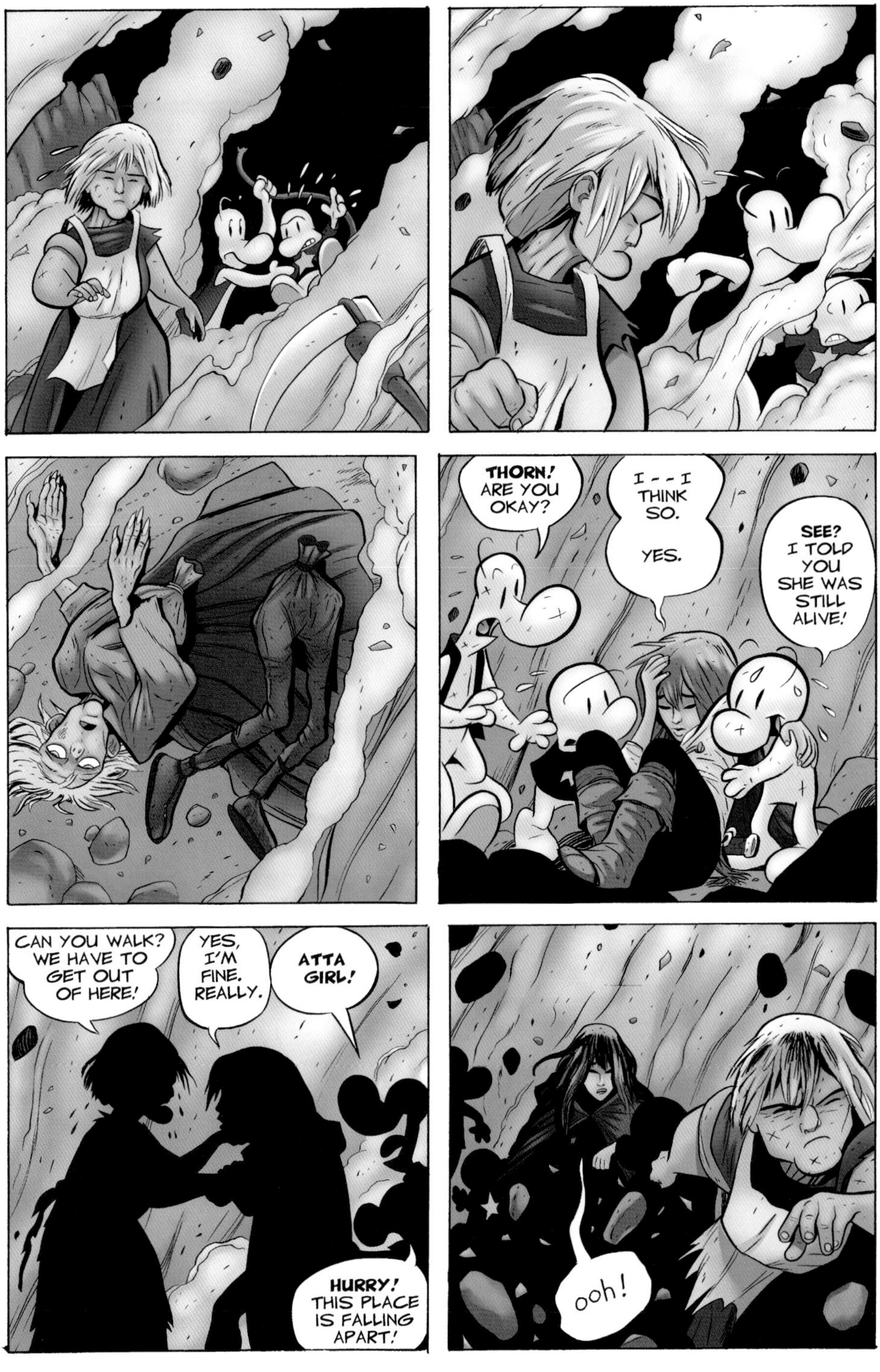
THORN! ARE YOU OKAY?
I -- I THINK SO.
YES.
SEE? I TOLD YOU SHE WAS STILL ALIVE!
CAN YOU WALK? WE HAVE TO GET OUT OF HERE!
YES, I'M FINE. REALLY.
ATTA GIRL!
HURRY! THIS PLACE IS FALLING APART!
ooh!

...TO BE CONTINUED.

About JEFF SMITH

JEFF SMITH was born and raised in the American Midwest and learned about cartooning from comic strips, comic books, and watching animated shorts on TV. After four years of drawing comic strips for The Ohio State University's student newspaper and co-founding Character Builders animation studio in 1986, Smith launched the comic book *BONE* in 1991. Between *BONE* and other comics projects, Smith spends much of his time on the international guest circuit promoting comics and the art of graphic novels.

More about *BONE*

An instant classic when it first appeared in the U.S. as an underground comic book in 1991, Bone has since garnered 38 international awards and sold a million copies in 15 languages. Now Scholastic's GRAPHIX imprint is publishing full-color graphic novel editions of the nine-book *BONE* series. Look for the continuing adventures of the Bone cousins in *Ghost Circles*.